TABLE OF CONTENTS

ACKNOWLEDGMENT AND AUTHOR'S NOTE

I do acknowledge the needed excellent assistance of Doreen Strait in making this book a reality.

I further acknowledge the many people to whom I said "Tell me a word and I will tell you a story". They inspired several of the short stories.

As the author, of course all errors are mine alone. I did randomly use a dictionary for 26 stories by selecting 26 words, defining them simply, and using that word as the theme for stories. I did, likewise for 13 stories, using a combination of two words and using both of them in those 13 stories. With regard to future books of short stories, I have several concepts, including 26 reincarnation stories; several hit woman stories; 13 other magic bracelet stories with the theme of "undoing one regret; and many others so that there will be one or more books of short stories utilizing the prime number 97 in the title.

It is my hope that readers will discover one or more short fiction stories that they can relate to and enjoy.

Donald W. Drueshobe

LAPIDARY

When he was four years old, Kevin was given a colorful book filled with pictures of beautiful stones and gems. This book detailed the origin of many stones and gems and provided the science and geography regarding them. It also set forth the history of famous gemstones. One section headed Lapidary showed how intricate that art skill was. One who was designated a lapidary expert had to intensely study the stone or gem to see where to cut it. Polishing the stone or gem was important but could be easily learned. The great skill was knowing where to cut and having the patience and artistry to do so.

He spent innumerable hours looking at the book; having it read to him and reading it to himself. He kept this book throughout his school years and when he was at college. He found a pocket size version of this book so he could take it easily with him. Kevin when he was thirteen years old found an expensive oversize edition of this book and bought it. In the city where Kevin lived there were two established jewelry stores (not including the mall large franchise jewelry stores). He worked in his senior year at one of the jewelry stores but lapidary was not performed there.

One of the highlights of his life was when each year a gemstone show came to town and Kevin could see first- hand the wondrous display of gemstones. A few times an old man who was a lapidarist would arrive. Kevin spent hours viewing the skill and artistry of the lapidary, Noah, and asked many questions. Kevin obtained a degree in fine art at college.

Kevin, after graduation, took a year off and went to Belgium and Holland and using the introduction from Noah, Kevin secured employment in a diamond and other fine gemstone firm where several highly trained and skilled lapidarists were employed. That year sealed Kevin's fate to be a lapidarist.

LAPIDARY

There he met Ingrid, who was one of the very few female lapidarists. Ingrid had worked with her three uncles and grandfather, who were acknowledged lapidarists since she was six years old. Ingrid saw in Kevin a true soul mate and she spent much time with him in private tutoring sessions.

During that year, he learned more about lapidary than he could have learned or experienced in many college years.

Kevin was allowed to study and cut gemstones and he had the thrill of his life when after several intense hours and days he received praise for his artistry and skill

Several of the lapidarists at the factory either died or retired and Kevin became in that short time, one of the most trusted lapidarists. Kevin and Ingrid spent their free time visiting museums, art galleries and gem shows.

A week before Kevin was to go back to the United States ad to start seeking employment in his chosen career, he saw a brilliant emerald gemstone in its raw unstudied uncut state. Kevin s asked if he wanted to extend his visa and be the lead lapidarist in cutting this emerald gemstone.

He met Ingrid that evening and told her about the once in a lifetime offer. Ingrid urged Kevin to do this. Kevin proposed to Ingrid saying "I Love You. I love everything about you." "Together we can make history in lapidary."

Ingrid said "sure" and Kevin with help and encouragement from her, intensely studied and then cut the raw emerald gemstone in such a way that four lovely emerald gems perfect in every way were produced.

Kevin and Ingrid were married with Kevin giving Ingrid a superb emerald engagement ring and they each proudly wore silver wedding rings. Eventually Kevin and Ingrid acquired the most respected lapidary firm in Europe. They did not have a fairy tale marriage except in their dreams, but a real marriage. Three children were born, Zachary, Bianca, and Suzette, but none of them were really interested in lapidary. Kevin and Ingrid always thought "well, we will wait and perhaps one of our grandchildren will love lapidary the way we do."

OPTION

Karen and Brian were in the apartment rented by Karen and had agreed to meet and discuss their options. They had been dating exclusively for the past seven months and found that they had similar values; were compatible in most ways; enjoyed their relationship including sex.

One option was to be engaged and married. The problems of that option were that they knew this would alienate both of their families because both sets of parents and all close relatives have been bitter enemies for many years. The cause was that a lucrative business venture fell through for both sets of parents which if successful would have made them very wealthy. For good reasons, each side believes the other side deliberately prevented such success.

Brian and Karen had lied by omission to their parents about their relationship and this has proved to be destructive to their relationship and option for future happiness.

Both Brian and Karen were beholden for financial support. Each had graduated from college and were actively pursuing advanced degrees, with Brian in a multi-disciplinary Master's degree program and Karen pursuing a specialized MBA program.

Neither had any separate financial resources available. Brian and Karen readily acknowledged they did not have a passionate love for one another but both believed that they had a mature love which would endure.

The other option they had was to continue to deceive the parents and enjoy their relationship but each was in an emotional state where such deception would be impossible.

Siblings of both Brian and Karen were arriving in a week to stay with them while exploring their options for college.

After much discussion they agreed their best and only option was to not see each other and to continue their separate education and when completed find some financial security in their professions and then marry.

OPTION

They tried to have an enjoyable rest of the evening but could not do so. For the following four months they never saw each other; nor called the other; and never communicated in any manner. Brian and Karen did go to the same university but since this was a large institution, each went to classes in separate buildings. Each thought they saw each other on the vast campus but never waved nor spoke.

Brian while hurrying across a busy intersection was struck by a vehicle and was taken to the university Hospital and was in intensive care. At about the same time, Karen suffered a serious gall bladder attack and was in intensive care at the same hospital. One of the nurses told each of them "What a strange situation, to have two graduate students from the same university in intensive care at the same time." The nurse used their first names. Brian and Karen were able to talk to each other and during the days in ICU they reached the conclusion that they have been foolish to stay away from one another and their only option for the future when released to move in together to take care of each other physically and emotionally.

Each made a clean breast of this situation to their parents and stated emphatically the only option for both families was to accept their relationship or disown them and the children they would have in the future. These would be the first grandchildren. Within a short time, the parents and siblings accepted this option. Brian and Karen did marry and had three children. The animosity between the two sets of parents lessened and finally disappeared completely when two of the children of Brian's parents, Sally and Ervin married two of the children of Karen's parents, Steven and Axil.

Over the years there were many festive family occasions. Within reason these were happy times and resulted from the option chosen by Karen and Brian.

NEE

Grandfather Isaac, the head of the family bellowed, "Jeremy, you will revoke your engagement to marry with Julia today. This is my order."

The family was gathered together at the demand of Isaac. Jeremy's parents, Richard and Jessica, said "That is not fair. Jeremy and Julia have been engaged for six months and the wedding is set at the Church in two months." Jeremy said, "I am 26 years old, employed as a computer specialist, and I love Julia."

Isaac repeated his edict and said, "Everyone knows it is a mortal sin against our religion and our culture that Julia requires that upon marriage she will keep her maiden name." The response was that Julia has a professional career under her "Nee" name and it would be of no benefit to her to change her name when married. It was pointed out that many marriages result in a hyphenated name. There have been a few instances where the husband uses the last name of the wife.

Isaac repeated his mantra that Julia must change her name to that of Jeffrey or the marriage is a nullity. Isaac then used the children argument—What names are the children to have?   Jeffrey responded that the children would have his surname, and further that Julia fully agrees.

Isaac was then asked what he would do-Not go to the wedding—act as though Julia does not exist; shun Julia and the children? Isaac left the room muttering to himself but provided one more drama saying "Your marriage will fall since it sis cursed." Jeffrey and his parents shook their heads in disbelief. Jeffrey met Julia and related this latest outburst and edict of Isaac. Julia liked Isaac and asked Jeffrey if she should have a discussion with Isaac but Jeffrey said this would be futile and maybe time would allow Isaac to see his error. However, Isaac stuck to his theme and on several occasions reiterated his view point. This stubborn attitude of Isaac placed a pall over what should have been a joyous event. As far as possible, Isaac was excluded from the events before the wedding. At the insistence of Julia, Isaac was invited to the family dinner scheduled four days before the wedding and was invited to both the wedding and reception.

NEE

Isaac preferred to be stubborn and even handwrote a letter to Jeffrey and Julia stating in the starkest of terms his viewpoint. Isaac expected that Jeffrey and Julia would give in on this "Nee" name issue but that did not occur. Isaac did come to the dinner, wedding and reception and loudly expressed his edict.

At the wedding care was taken to emphasize that Julia would retain her maiden name upon the marriage. Isaac never relented nor apologized and upon his death, showed his detestation for this matter by excluding Jeffrey and Julia and any children they ever would give birth to from a having any share of his wealth. In his will, Isaac specifically restated in the most dire of words his belief that Julia by retaining her maiden name doomed the marriage to Jeffrey and that the marriage would be cursed.

Isaac went so far as to pay for a newspaper insertion reiterating for the community to read his viewpoint. The family was embarrassed but Julia with Jeffrey solidly backing her throughout her life was known by her maiden name.

METHOD

Ken, thinking to himself, thought "Method—how I can kill Louis and not get caught". "He is my only brother-in-law and I hate him for trying to hurt badly, my sister, Nanci, and their two children, Tommy and Ariste." "The last straw was when Nanci had an accident last week when her brakes failed." "I know Louis did something to the brakes but so far the police are only "investigating".

Nanci, due to her skills as a driver, was able to have a not very severe collision but did have three broken ribs; a mild concussion; and now fear for her life and safety and the safety of the children.

If Nanci had been disabled, Louis would have followed through and secured custody of the children and their nightmare would start anew. So far, Louis only had strict supervised visits with the children and this would continue until the scheduled custody trial before the Judge in two months.

Ken wished that his and Nanci's parents were still alive but they died several years ago. Ken said to himself that he was the only one who could protect and save Nanci and the children. Ken did not want any real chance in killing Louis that he would be convicted since how could he protect those he loved if he was in prison. Louis had some relatives and cronies who might seek revenge if Louis was murdered and Ken was the main suspect.

Ken had ruled out shooting Louis since Ken had no firearm skills. Also ruled out were knives or a club since in a one on one situation between Ken and Louis, Louis might prevail. Ken knew little about poison. It would be good if Louis died in an accident or fall or a fatal fire but Ken did not know enough to stage such an accident.

Ken had been agonizing over this problem which was now of even more urgency due to the fear that Louis would try to kill Nanci again.

Ken although he had many friends did not want to involve them in any way. A new real fear for Ken was that Nanci may have reached her breaking point and would regardless of consequences try to or succeed in killing Louis herself.

METHOD

Ken having discarded the most obvious methods of killing Louis thought "Maybe there is a way to get Louis convicted and imprisoned for a crime Louis either had committed or for which he could be blamed."

Louis was a sports gambler and often was in serious trouble with bookies but recently so he claimed he had become a consistent winner.

Suddenly, Ken remembered that a body of a young girl had recently been discovered after ten years. Ken knew police officers and had learned they had found a cigarette lighter under the body with DNA on the lighter mixed with a little blood of the victim. The DNA sample would prove the identity without question but the problem was that DNA sample had not found any match in the databases.

Ken asked to see the lighter and was shown by one of his police friends a detailed photo of the lighter. Ken believed he had seen Louis with a quite similar lighter many years ago. The police had no success in tracing this old lighter since it was a common brand and sold in the millions. Ken knew it would be unwise for many reasons to directly point a finger at Louis.

Ken decided to use an untraceable throwaway cell phone and bought on the internet a voice disguising device. Ken called two police officers and relayed information that Louis did have a similar lighter near the time of the death of the girl. Ken also said there should be a nick on the right corner of the lighter and further that Louis soon after the date the girl was killed bought a brand new similar lighter.

The police and district attorney secured a probable cause warrant and searched Louis and found the same kind of lighter. Since Louis was arrested, he had his cheeks swabbed for a DNA test. The DNA test proved a match and Louis was charged with first degree murder. Since he was in county prison waiting for trial, the Custody trial was postponed and supervised visitation was revoked. Louis became convinced he had no chance and pleaded guilty and was sentenced to 25 years in prison.

METHOD

Ken was relieved that this problem was solved and that he could finally quit thinking of a new method to kill Louis or at least until Louis was released from prison. Nanci secured an uncontested divorce from Louis.

BLACKLIST

In the 1950's, Jerry came home to his wife Lily in midday and told her he was fired from his job. They had been married for over two years and were expecting their first child in six months. Jerry had worked as an accountant for the firm since graduation. Legally he was an at-will employee and he could be let go without cause. Jerry was in shock and could not understand why he was fired. He planned to apply for unemployment compensation but knew he would, if deemed eligible, only receive 2/3 of his regular pay. Lily did have a part- time job and had no chance to increase her hours or pay.

Within a day both Jerry and Lily told their parents and relatives. They received unsolicited advice to sue but knew this was not feasible.

Jerry applied for unemployment compensation and the accounting firm did not contest this. He applied to the other accounting firms in the area but was given no interview.

Jerry had long thought about opening his own accounting and tax office but the start up cost was beyond their means and financial resources.

David, a former fellow employee met Jerry for a lunch and told him that Jerry was on a blacklist since a suspicion arose from his involvement when he was in college of membership in an organization that was believed to be affiliated with maybe a radical group which might be working to change a certain south American country which was controlled by a military dictatorship and was anti-democracy.

Jerry remembered going to a few meetings because his now wife, then girlfriend, Lily, was friends with two people who had fled that South American country and sought asylum in the United States. Jerry never joined this group officially but did believe in justice and democracy.

Jerry went back to two firms that he thought he had a chance to be employed but was not considered employable due to being on the blacklist.

BLACKLIST

Jerry and Lily did have a conference with a lawyer who was sympathetic but told them there was no specific law relating to blacklisting. Richard, the attorney, told them that Senator Joseph McCarthy and others were "rooting" out communists and the political climate in the United States was hardcore vs. any subversive suspected groups. Richard gave his best advice was for them to move and seek employment elsewhere. Neither Jerry nor Lily had any martyr desires.

Jerry did open an accounting practice in his home and sought out former clients. With a great deal of effort and work, Jerry over the years did succeed in his accounting profession but he always knew how much he had lost in time and money due to being unfairly blacklisted.

KICKBACK

Sophia was a junior executive at music recording company. Sophia believed her long time boyfriend was going to ask her to marry him when Dick called urgently to see her the evening before Valentine Day. They met at a trendy small restaurant and each ordered only coffee. Sophia thought this was a problem since Dick usually immediately ordered a meal and dessert but thought maybe he was nervous.

Dick said, "This is the hardest thing I have ever done. Yesterday I became engaged to Rosalie and we are to be married tomorrow at City Hall. Initially, I was not going to tell you until it was completed but I thought I do not want to be a coward. We had a very good relationship and I at one time believed you were the one for me but life and true love intervened."

"I wish you only the best, Sophia." Still in shock, she gathered her wits and told Dick "Congratulations-I do wish you well. Goodbye" and she left holding back her sorrow and tears.

Sophia decided to not put her heart out anymore and to turn her energy to being a great employee. For the next eight months, Sophia was a dynamo at work and was promoted. Sophia did not date and had no desire to be hurt again.

Sophia who arrived at work early, rarely left for lunch, and stayed late, became curious as to how a band she thought was mediocre at best was getting plush gigs and extra special recording studio time.

On her own time she investigated and found clear evidence of a sophisticated kickback scheme between this band, its manager and three fellow employees. Sophia carefully over time, gathered all the evidence, made duplicate copies and rented a safe deposit box at a local bank.

She also consulted a knowledgeable attorney, Sam, and received advice at how to best go forward as a whistle blower. She was furious that the best job she ever had was being destroyed by this kickback scheme.

KICKBACK

Sophia met with the CEO and other executives and laid out all the evidence. The executives were appalled but wanted to cover up this kickback scheme and quietly fire the employees. Sophia objected and sought justice. Sophia reported this scheme to the FBI and other federal government agencies and also revealed all to a friendly newspaper person.

The story broke and suddenly at many record companies similar kickback schemes were uncovered. It turned out that this type of kickback was rampant and actually well known and had been concealed for years. In some circles she was praised and in others damned. Sophia had to quit her job. Sophia did receive a substantial reward (which was taxable by IRS at ordinarily income tax rates) and she was a media star for a time.

Sophia spent over two years researching the kickback problem and wrote two books which were best sellers. Sophia also went on the lecture circuit and enjoyed a public speaking career.

Sophia over the years became an expert on Kickback schemes in many media areas. Sophia never had a romantic encounter again and lived with her anti-kickback stance and fame seemingly happy.

JIVE

The five of them had been friends during the school years. None of them went to college or to trade schools. They were each 25 years old and partially settled. None were married nor in a live-in situation. Three of them had romantic liaisons. Roger was a clerk in a media store and was dating Sybil. George had a job in a grocery chain store and was dating Ruth. Brenda was a legal secretary and was dating Mark. The last two, Nathan and Cheryl, had not dated anyone recently and all of a sudden they saw each other with a fresh viewpoint. Nathan was a musician and performed in a band. Cheryl had discovered that she could sing and in addition to her day job in a shoe store did sing at gigs.

Cheryl had found jive band music in her attic and had at once taken these to Nathan. Nathan did take these jive music albums to his band and told them that Jive was more of a swinging music and led to the jazz era. All had heard of jazz musicians and one of the most famous Jazz singers, Etta James. On the side they started to play the jive music and soon knew they needed a singer.

Nathan talked to Cheryl and convinced her to come to the jive jam sessions. Cheryl wanted to enhance her singing career and did come. Soon the band with Cheryl singing jive tunes appeared in public venues as a jive band.

About six months later they were playing at a hotel and a music entrepreneur was in the audience. His name was Albert. He contacted Nathan, Cheryl and the band and offered a tryout with his record company to do jive songs and an album. Albert had a great deal of influence in the music industry. Soon Nathan and Cheryl and the other band members quit their day jobs and were touring to selected venues. This was a slow process to in effect revive Jive in the very crowded music scene but in four years they were successful. In addition to live touring, they did three well-received albums of jive music. Their music was danceable and lively.

JIVE

This Jive band stayed together and they all came to love Jive as s music genre and it brought some fame and fortune to all of them. They did not win any of the music awards but knew that Jive music was fulfilling their deep need to be different and proud.

Two years before Nathan and Cheryl found that they were more than compatible and did marry.

Nathan and Cheryl cut back on the touring and devoted more time to the recording studio to make jive music and succeeded.

Nathan and Cheryl had twins, and they had pet nicknames for them, Jive and Jazz—the two Js. The real names of the children were Axil and Belinda, their two daughters.

IMMOBILE

As a result of the combination of severe nerve damage to her spine and various psychological trauma, Arid, was immobile. She could not move to any significant degree her arms, or her legs. She breathed satisfactorily. Her brain was fully functioning. Arid could move her head with great effort a few inches to each side and up and down. Arid could eat and drink with some effort. Arid did possess a full range of speech.

Arid was 26 and had been immobile for over seven years. Her health insurance was nearing depletion due to lifetime caps. Arid survived on SSI of about $600.00 per month.

Arid still had her parents, Ruth and Robert, with whom she lived but they were both retired and tired. Several charitable agencies provided people support for Arid. Over the years, Arid had well more than fifteen minutes of fame. Arid had been examined and studied by brain specialists; spinal experts; psychologists; and neurologists. All agreed her injuries were real but had no clear explanation why Arid was immobile.

Unexpectedly, one day a woman, Sybil, about 55 years old, and her son, Carl, a respected photographer, aged 26, came to visit Arid. Initially Sybil and Carl wanted to write a biography of Arid, and to do a photo spread. Arid was receptive but cautious and wondered what could be said and portrayed about her that would make her story memorable.

Sybil with Carl backing her up said "Give us six weeks and obey everything we say to do and you will not be immobile. You will walk normally and use your arms and have all possible movement."

Arid responded "How is that possible? I have been immobile for seven years; have had six operations; have been studied and examined by excellent doctors."

Carl said, "When I was three years old, for a year I was likewise immobile and no cause nor cure could be found but one night I heard three words clearly uttered – Believe-Trust-Love."

IMMOBILE

Carl and Sybil explained that they had made it both their mission and passion to find those who were immobile and utilizing this verbal therapy to "cure" such immobility, whatever the cause or reason for it.

Sybil and Carl presented newspaper and other media tales of some seventeen immobile people, adults and children, so "cured". All ceased to be immobile and remained mobile.

Arid said she was desperate and would try anything and would willingly without reservations do whatever Sybil and Carl advocated for the next six weeks. Arid asked what the cost would be and was told there was zero cost. Arid only had to willingly "believe-trust-love" and this would work.

Arid could withdraw within herself and go into a daydream trance and she did so while Sybil and Carol waited.

During this time which in real time lasted for exactly 73 seconds, Arid stayed in such state and when she came "awake" Arid told Sybil and Carl that she did "Believe-Trust-Love".

Sybil and Carl came to visit Arid periodically during the next six weeks. Two days before the end of that six week time, Arid not only had full range of movement of her head but for the first time could move her arms freely and then walked with no difficulty. Carl had taken many photographs of Arid during those six weeks and took a video of her ceasing to be immobile. Sybil had discussed at great length with Arid her life story, her immobility; her thoughts and feeling.

Sybil and Carl published to some acclaim their story of Arid and her recovery. Alas, due to skepticism in the medical, psychological, and scientific communities, there was wide spread decision to ridicule and down play the recovery of Arid and the book did not attain best seller status and was read by few.

Sybil and Carl continued with their life work of seeking out immobile persons and without any monetary reward helping such persons to become mobile.

IMMOBILE

Arid remained mobile; did successfully obtain a Master's degree in Counseling; did have a good career in Counseling; did get married and had three children (in her heart she named them Believe-Trust-Love).

HUMID

There is disbelief in "climate change" despite all the scientific evidence that this is occurring. One of the problems is that those believing sincerely in climate change often go to extremes in examples and predictions. It would be far better to be "conservative" and to down play to some limited extent the probable result of climate change. When the most dire predictions do not happen or are not as bad as predicted then many people become non-believers.

It is now the year 2024 and some of the direst of predictions have occurred. More people and countries have started slowly to do something about pollution, etc.

However for the average person in the United States like the family consisting of father, Louis, 36, an accountant; his wife of 11 years, Betty, age 35 a part time school teacher; and their three children Rose, age 9, George, age 7-1/2, and Sue, age 4, life in the city is terrible.

Betty, George, and Sue have serious health problems such as asthma, allergies and respiratory medical matters.

Louis has good health insurance coverage so there is not a serious financial problem.

Louis and Betty have discussed moving to a better climate for the health of the family and Louis can relocate since he works for a nationwide firm. The real problem is that almost all areas of the United States are very humid due in large measure to climate change.

For example, most of Arizona is 50% more humid year around than was true just three years before and the humidity index is steadily rising not just by a small percentage but by percentages whereby the humidity levels will double about every six years. The only relief is to stay in air conditioned homes with special expensive humidity controls; travel in modified humidity lessened vehicles; work in offices or factories so equipped. The initial cost of such equipment is increasing the same way, doubling every six years or less. The cost of electricity and other energy sources likewise are doubling every four years.

HUMID

Some people are spending more for such humidity equipment than the cost of a new vehicle. Most people are spending more per year re: humidity than their mortgage.

The federal government in order to provide subsidies for all re: humidity related matters has imposed a surcharge on all income, including earned income; interest; dividends; capital gains; and to lesser extent on what is called "unrealized appreciation" on all assets. Crash expensive programs have reduced unemployment to the vanishing point since so many are employed re: humidity projects.

In the last few years strict price controls have been mandated on all health care.

Betty and Louis finally settled on relocating to an island area in the Pacific where many are fleeing since there is very little humidity present. It is still viable to move there because the cost of living is low; and these islands are seeking families with young children. Betty and Louis decided that this was the only chance their children had to escape the horror of humidity and they did move there.

GALLOP

Sally, 16 years old, had been riding horses for over 12 years when she had her life threatening skiing accident. Sally was a good skier but when she doing so, two young men who were racing each other collided with her causing her to go off trail and she hit a tree. The next thing Sally knew it was three days later and she was in a hospital bed with her left leg in a complete cast. Her left leg was broken above and below her knew and her ankle was severely injured.

As she lay in the bed at the hospital she remembered the thrill of the gallop when she cut loose with her favorite horse, Cyclone. She recalled the first time she rode Cyclone and how fast this horse seemed to be. "Oh, the thrill of the gallop that was!" thought Sally.

Sally had loving parents, Ralph and Cara, and two brothers, Zack and Jim, and one sister a year younger, Georgia. They regularly came to see her in the hospital and when she was transferred to a rehab center.

By the time she had as much recovery as could be done, it was May and Sally would usually be riding Cyclone, her horse, most weekends. Sally had to do intensive work to catch up at school so she could ultimately graduate with her class so she focused on school work and was back in high school. Sally was a popular girl at school but now felt self-conscious about her left leg and the difficulty she had walking. Sally had been told that her left leg due to severe injuries would never be the same. Sally had rejected amputation of her left leg.

On a bright day in June, Sally decided to try to ride Cyclone. The first time, Sally rode Cyclone and it was totally different since she had no strength in her left leg. Cyclone seemed to know that Sally had problems and proceeded to at most trot with a simple gait. Sally wanting to test herself urged Cyclone to gallop and when Cyclone did, Sally fell off (for the first time ever) and seriously re-injured her left leg. Sally spent the months of June and July in the rehab center.

GALLOP

Sally did a great deal of thinking while laying in bed at the rehab facility and came to the conclusion that she was not going to let her skiing accident and her left leg define her or control her life.

The first weekend after she was discharged, Sally went to ride Cyclone again. She initially rode at a slow pace but then urged Cyclone to gallop. This time, Sally did not fall and controlled the gallop. Sally continued to ride Cyclone and usually rode at a gallop.

FIXTURE

Ceasar and Michelle, after six years of marriage, decided to be divorced. At that time, Ceasar was 30 and Michelle was 29. They were employed with Ceasar being the assistant manager at a retail store and Michelle being a clerk at an insurance agency. Two years prior they had bought a modest home and it was heavily mortgaged. Neither had wanted children and that was not the reason for the divorce. Both were reasonable regarding money matters. Neither had any interest in anyone at the time of their decision to divorce. There had never been abuse. They seemed to have an angry dispute about a myriad of otherwise trivial matters. Both felt tired and worn down trying to meet each other's expectations.

Quite simply, even if in fact they initially married for love their personalities were not compatible. They often wished that there was some major issue to be angry and disturbed about but there was none.

Often each of them thought as a simile that their marriage started out as fully inflated tire and slowly the air leaked out so that they were driving their marriage on not just one flat tire but all four tires were flat. They both knew there was no future and probably never was for them as a couple.

They both wanted to part company on friendly terms. There was no basis for any alimony and each did have employer health insurance coverage.

There home was in a good location so it sold rapidly. They had 30 days to remove all their furniture and personal items as part of the agreement of sale.

Both Ceasar and Michelle were noted for being stubborn and to some extent willful. They had agreed in writing on how to divide most furniture items and personal property but there still remained some that were in dispute. They knew that the compactor was a fixture which stayed in the home but Michelle really loved that compactor but was finally convinced to leave it.

FIXTURE

There were four items which each wanted to keep despite the fact that none of them were of particular value in monetary terms. The first was an elaborate Christmas ornament that they both adored which was a gift from a five year old nephew of Michelle who pooled his money with the six year old niece of Ceasar to have that ornament created.

The second was a set of small teacups bought when they were on vacation and happy. The third was an old print of a landscape that meant something of value to each of them. The fourth item was an embroidered small wall hanging that each believed important for different reasons.

Even though it turned out that there were no substantial disputes other than ownership of those four items they were wise to have separate lawyers, Charles and Vince. The attorneys had made it easy to resolve other issues which could have derailed the friendly divorce. However, since each wanted all four items and was more than willing to pay the other, after several meetings someone had to either surrender or else they might have to go through litigation which would take much time, effort and expense. Division of all marital property was under the divorce code to be equitable but there were no court cases or regulations to provide any certainty with respect to dividing or possession of in effect sentimental personal property.

Both attorneys told Caesar and Michelle that there were only a few alternatives:

1. Donate all four items to a charity.
2. Destroy all four items.
3. Have a sealed written bid with the highest one acquiring all four items or a sealed bid for each item. This was logical and reasonable method to resolve this issue.

4. Since none of the items were fixtures that are attached to the home, leaving them for the new owners was not legal or required but leaving them was an option.

5. The more creative attorney, Vince, came up with a solution that both Ceasar and Michelle agreed to. Since they both liked games they were persuaded to have four pages with each item on one page and pin them on a cork board. Then both Caesar and Michelle would be blindfolded and spun around similar to the kid game of "pin the tail on the donkey". They would use two darts each to pin two papers each resulting in owning those pinned items.

They were both weary of this dispute and on the last day before the removal of furniture and personal property was required they did this fun endeavor. The result was that Michelle pinned the tea cup set and wall hanging pages with Caesar pinning the Christmas ornament and the landscape print pages.

Each were happy with the result but in some ways sad to see their marriage end. However they would always have the exhilarating hilarious memory of being a child again and playing a silly game.

Michelle and Ceasar gave each other a fierce hug and expressed their sincere wish that each would find true happiness in their future. And they meant it.

ESCHEW

Soon after she turned three, Rosalie one day surprised her parents, Larry and Carol, by clearly stating the word "eschew". Rosalie asked what does eschew mean. Her parents always tried to answer her and said the dictionary states that eschew means "to keep away from or to avoid". Rosalie was satisfied and often used the word eschew. As the year progressed Rosalie continued to surprise and delight her parents by asking them to tell her the dictionary meaning of many words. In one week span Rosalie inquired as to the meaning of prolific — dalliance — euphoric — oddball — capitalist — shameful — observant — cautious — absentism — and devious.

Each time the parents satisfied the curiosity of Rosalie. Rosalie used all those unusual words in her everyday speech and surprised relatives and others with her precise accurate pronunciations of such words and using them in complete sentences with accuracy. Rosalie also had a journal and she carefully wrote correctly all these words. Rosalie had learned to read by age three and on occasion was found with the dictionary opened she was reading the meaning of many words.

Rosalie entered school for truly gifted students and graduated from high school at age 14 and had a PhD in language by the time she was 22. Rosalie throughout her life astounded all with the extent of her vocabulary and command of language. Rosalie became the youngest fully tenured professor in history and wrote many books which were used both in high school and universities worldwide. She won many awards for excellence and was admired by all who knew her or heard her speak.

Rosalie did get married and lived a happy life having children, grandchildren, and great-grandchildren.

Rosalie always gave great praise to her parents. Rosalie did write a book of poetry and used as its title "eschew" not because that word was relevant to the poems but because she always remembered the first unusual word she said.

DRAGNET

By a coincidence, Ashley was waiting when she was at the police station for her boyfriend, secretly her fiancé, Tim, to finish his shift when she heard the all points bulletin:

"APB – be on the lookout for Ashley –she is blond, has blue eyes – is 5 ft. 5 in. tall and is about 124 lbs. – she has a mole below her left eye and a cleft chin—she is wanted for abetting a foiled bank robbery—she may be armed and is considered dangerous—she is between 24 and 29 years old—approach with caution."

Ashley fit all those descriptive attributes except her mole was near her right eye. Ashley thought to herself "Here we go, again—last year it was identity theft by this other Ashley and it took me six months to untangle my credit card and store credit cards mess." Ashley was never caught but maybe this time she will be since this is a State wide dragnet.

A few minutes later, Tim came into the police station and immediately hugged Ashley telling her to be very careful that she did not get picked up in this dragnet.

Since this was serious Ashley waited with Tim till she could see the Chief of Police. When they went into his office, Rodney, the police chief had his deputy, Aaron, and two FBI agents were there. Their names were John and Jon.

It was explained to Ashley that until this dragnet was over and the bad Ashley caught that she, the good Ashley, was in serious danger of being mistaken for the bad Ashley with dire consequences. Ashley knew this and asked what she should do.

Ashley was told that she should go into protective custody and let her family and employer (she was for four years a Bond investment analyst) and let them know the situation. It appeared that there was no option which would allow Ashley to live and act in a normal way until bad Ashley was captured. Even then Ashley knew she could have a lasting stigma.

DRAGNET

Ashley wondered if the two Ashleys were twins separated at birth due to the fact that their descriptions were almost identical. Ashley thought of changing her first name and toyed with the name of Judith but she also realized she had to change her hair color; get dull contacts even though she did not need eyeglasses and to go to the extreme yet serious cosmetic surgery to really change her face.

Neither Ashley nor Tim wanted those severe changes. Ashley did call her employer and said she could work with her laptop etc. without going to the office and that was agreeable. Her parents, Jim and Sue, were dismayed, but recognized how serious this was.

Tim and Ashley had been secretly engaged for the past month and they briefly contemplated a swift marriage but decided that they were not going to let bad Ashley control their lives. On a temporary basis it was agreed that Tim would move in with Ashley. No one believed that Ashley was in any danger from bad Ashley but was in danger of being mistaken by the police, etc. searching diligently for bad Ashley.

Some five days later during what would be a routine traffic stop, bad Ashley along with the driver, Ken, were
shot.

Neither Ashley, the criminal, nor Ken were severely wounded but were taken under guard to the hospital.

Ashley and Tim attended the trial of bad Ashley and Ken and they were found guilty and sentenced to lengthy prison time.

Ashley did change the color of her hair to a reddish tint and altered her hair style. Ashley had the mole near her right eye removed. She also reversed her first and middle names and had that name change court approved. Thereafter, her name was Judith Ashley but she went by Judith A.

DRAGNET

Ashley and Tim were married and the now Judith was fully aware that when and if bad Ashley was released from prison that this identity situation might rise again but Judith A. being an optimist always remembered her good fortune of being in the police station of all places when the dragnet for bad Ashley started.

APIARY

Stella, a 34 year old divorcee, worked in an apiary for the past two years. She had not only a legal shared custody arrangement with her former husband, Albert, relating to their two children, Zeke, and Ariel, 11 and 9 years old, but shared physical custody. Each would have the children for a week. This custodial situation which had been in place for over four years worked out well. They lived shout two miles away from one another. They each had supportive families. They shared when school was in session a caretaker for the children paying one-half of the cost. They had found the way to be generous if either needed help. Since they earned close to the same amount of income, no child support order was needed. They shared holidays and vacation times. They each claimed one child as a dependent with regard to income tax. They were always amicable regarding the children and shared in the varied activities of the children. Neither Stella nor Albert had remarried or created a live-in situation. Each dated but only casually.

Albert, 35, was a botanist who taught botany at the local university. Albert for the past year had been studying the causes of the bee collapse. Stella, was even more concerned because she actively cared for hives and bees.

Neither Zeke nor Ariel wanted to do anything with bees. Zeke had an allergy whereby he was in some danger if stung by bees or other flying insect. Ariel one time was endangered when swarmed by seemingly angry wasps and had a real fear of bees, etc.

Stella and Albert had many interesting conversations with regard to bees and Albert had visited several times the Apiary where Stella worked. At least once a week, Stella had to deliver bees to nearby farms including fruit and berry farms.

On occasion, Albert came with Stella so he could observe the bees in action when they were pollinating trees, fruit, berries, and vegetables. Albert was working with several students in this study and preparing a paid for by grant report.

APIARY

When Stella during their marriage discussed the apiary/bee position, Albert criticized Stella since she had by that time a Master's degree in Biology and could have secured a teaching position at the University. Stella responded that she had always had a love for bees and was happiest when doing physical work with the bees and hives.

During the eight months that Albert was studying bee collapse with while going with Stella and being with her at her employment, Albert realized how wrong he was in overly criticizing Stella.

Albert was more sensitive to bee stings than Stella was and Stella constantly warned Albert of danger; attended to his on the few times he was actually stung. Albert had no serious reaction to these bee sting events but really appreciated the care given him by Stella.

Albert asked Stella to take a chance and to date him by going to dinners, movies, and going to family events together. Stella, believing that Albert was sincere and did regret his overt criticism of Stella, which in part led to their separation and divorce, agreed.

Albert and Stella dated and found that each of them saw in the other kindred feelings. The children were very happy to see the parents they adored together again.

After six months and about the time the bee collapse report was finished, Stella asked Albert what he was waiting for and remarked that time was passing and they were growing older. Albert took the "hint" and proposed to Stella.

They were married at the Apiary with the bees excluded. No one was stung. The reception was at a nearby hotel. There was no bee motif or reference at the wedding or receptions except for the favors for the guests were small bottles of honey produced from the apiary where Stella worked and where she recently became an active financial partner.

APIARY

The unknown future did occur and less than two years later, twins arrived the usual way. Albert wanted to name the girl Bee and the boy Hive but Zeke and Ariel (with assist from Stella) nixed that idea. The twins were named Bliss and Dare. The apiary thrived but bee collapse still was an unsolved mystery.

CENT

Howard, now 28 years old, never married, started saving U.S. Coins when he was five years old. He recalled finding one shiny cent on the floor and he carefully placed that cent in a mason jar.

From that day forward every time Howard found a coin; was given a coin; or had any coin in change, placed them in separate containers—one for cents—one for nickels—one for dimes—one for quarters. If Harold came into possession of a half dollar coin or a dollar coin he changed it for smaller coins.

Harold never spent any of the coins. Harold asked that if he was to receive money as a birthday or Xmas present that it be, if possible, in coins. Harold never cashed in paper money for coins but either spent this or eventually saved it. When Harold worked and cashed his paycheck, he saved the coins. When he paid cash for items, he always saved the coins he received in change. Harold seemed to have a sixth sense since he was constantly finding coins wherever he went. Harold continued this coin saving when he was in college and when he spent a year in the Peace Corps in Peru. If he received Peruvian coins he would exchange them for US coins and save them. Harold never had coin collection books and never made any effort to have any coin collection. For Harold this coin saving was for several distinct purposes and he had an objective for his savings of cents; nickels; dimes; and quarters. One secret goal that Harold had was his intention to be married by the time he reached thirty. Harold knew he had two years to achieve this.

Harold had dated but had never found any woman to focus on. Harold was an independent auto insurance agent for several years and was secure in his job and finances.

Harold had the following uses for his coin savings which he would use after his marriage to the presently unknown woman.

The quarters would be for a down payment when the time came to buy a house and he would continue saving quarters till that happened. Harold believed he had over $4,500.00 in saved quarters at present.

CENT

The dimes and nickels would suffice for new furniture sometime shortly after marriage and he knew he had over $4,000.00 saved in those coins. The cents being the most endearing to Harold would be used to buy an engagement ring and he had in excess of $2,000.00.

Harold often thought of the attributes of the woman who would be his lifetime mate: intelligent regardless of education; since Harold was 5 foot 10 inches tall, his wife should be between 5 foot three inches and five foot six inches tall; Harold wanted lively eyes and free flowing hair, with colors of little concern; the woman had to be trim and athletically disposed; Harold wanted a woman who shared his values or did not have serious conflicts with them. Harold wanted to find a woman who believed in optimism and trust and love. They could be opposites in many ways.

Harold also wanted his wife to want and love children but also to have true self-esteem and doing well at her job or career. Once, Harold had thought about all the attributes, he considered whether he would really want his wife to be never married before or would he accept her if divorced or widowed. Harold thought there would be few available widows so he limited his search to never married or divorcees in the age range of 21 to 27 since he wanted a younger wife.

For the next year and a half, Harold accelerated his dating situation but to no avail.

Harold had ruled out the co-workers he had at his place of employment and also other women who he knew in the auto insurance field.

About six months before Harold was thirty, he joined a fitness club and had good luck the first day there; he found three shiny cents on the floor near the machine he was using and believed this was a good omen.

CENT

A few days later, Harold as he was about to leave, heard a woman say, "look what I found. This is my lucky day." Harold was curious and he went to see what happened and found Lois, 25 years old, a registered nurse; examining a pouch filled with coins. Lois, in her excitement grabbed Harold and showed him her find. Harold pointed out that the bag had initials and told Lois, which she well knew anyway, to turn it in to the manger.

Harold went with Lois to do so and told Lois how he had found three cents earlier, Lois told Harold she saved coins and was always finding coins lying around.

Harold and Lois in unison asked each other to go out for breakfast and they did. Harold realized that Lois based on their conversation might be the one he was seeking to be his wife. Lois was attracted to Harold and she had never married. They talked about their love of children.

As they left the restaurant Lois spied two cents lying on the ground and each picked one up. Lois had a cent that was 29 years old and Harold had one exactly 25 years old. They started dating and soon fell in love.

Harold took the containers that had his cents to the bank and cashed them in and had $2,745.00 in a check. Harold went to the jeweler and picked out an engagement ring with the proviso that if Lois did not want that ring it could be readily exchanged for another. Harold met Lois outside the fitness center where they first met and asked Lois to take a real chance on love and marry him. Lois said, "Sure.". Lois did adore the engagement ring. Three days before Harold was thirty, they married. Harold used his coin savings for furniture and to partly provide a down payment on their first home.

Harold and Lois continued saving all coins that they received and used these coins savings to, in part, pay for college education for two of their three children. The third child opted to be a skilled carpenter) and the coin savings were used to provide that daughter with a very good set of tools.

Harold's slogan was "savings cents made sense".

ZUCCHINI

The Zucchini feud started at the county fair eight years ago. For many years, Aunt Bea, the oldest of the aunts by seven years, had won almost every year for her zucchini bread; her zucchini cake; her zucchini pastry; her zucchini salads. The rules were simple:

1. At least 60% of the item had to be made from natural zucchini.
2. The Judges had to find an actual zucchini taste and smell in the item.
3. There was no rule regarding shape or color or texture.
4. The winner in the judgement of the Judges had to have the best tasting, best smelling, and best presented zucchini item.

Aunt Bea had been the zucchini winner for many years except the year when close to cooking or baking time she suffered from recurrent diarrhea and failed to submit a zucchini item.

The other two aunts Aunt Charlotte and Aunt Dorothy never competed with Aunt Bea and were winners at the county fair for best rhubarb pie or best fine stitched doily, etc.

At a family party, several months before the county fair, Aunt Bea, more than somewhat tipsy, commenced to loudly proclaim that Aunts, Charlotte and Dorothy were afraid to compete regarding zucchini items and went on to brag that she was far superior and would to her dying day, always win with her famous zucchini items.

Both Aunt Dorothy and Aunt Charlotte were humiliated by this tirade and they agreed to work together to de-throne Aunt Bea.

ZUCCHINI

The families of each aunt then during the next eight years, sided with their aunt and many silly episodes occurred so that the three families became part of the feud. The main exception was Roger and Trudy, third cousins who loved each other; were engaged; and married in the early years of the feud. Their wedding was marred by an eruption by Aunt Dorothy who spilled a fruit cup on Aunt Bea. The two aunts had to be restrained. Roger and Trudy were embarrassed by this outrageous conduct and this event enhanced the feud.

The most recent situation involved second cousins Angela and Karen who announced at a family affair that they were in love with each other. They announced they planned to marry a week after the county fair since their State had fully approved gay marriage. Many of the extended families were shocked and dismayed but several supported Angela and Karen including Roger and Trudy. All three aunts were appalled and turned away from Angela and Karen establishing their bigotry.

Over the seven years of the zucchini feud, Aunt Bea won three times, Aunt Dorothy once, and Aunt Charlotte won the other three years.

The winning zucchini items were; zucchini bread; zucchini pie; zucchini cake; zucchini salad; zucchini sherbert; zucchini ice cream; exotic varieties of a zucchini blended into a shake.

The eighth county fair was to do or die between Aunt Bea and Aunt Charlotte so that the tie would end.

Each of the aunts had serious ailments and had been hospitalized often. Aunt Bea was 89, Aunt Dorothy was 82, and Aunt Charlotte was 80. Aunt Charlotte had serious diabetic and gall bladder problems. Aunt Dorothy had two heart attacks and had high blood pressure and bad cholesterol. Aunt Bea suffered from gout and had illnesses regarding obesity and also had substantial gum disease.

All three believe this would be the last county fair they would submit zucchini items and all wanted to go out in glory and fame.

ZUCCHINI

Aunt Bea, using all the secret recipes prepared an exotic zucchini bread which had the texture and flavor and smell of a fluffy cake.

Aunt Dorothy using combinations of several different zucchinis and mixing in many herbs and spices prepared a very tasty salad.

Aunt Charlotte made zucchini cupcakes.

There were five judges who took an extended time to taste and feel and smell the zucchini entries. The cupcakes were very tasty and had an aroma which was unique.

The judges were unanimous in awarding Aunt Charlotte the gold ribbon.

The public was treated to the cupcakes and within an hour after the gold ribbon was awarded to Aunt Charlotte several said the secret was that the cupcakes were filled with distilled marijuana. The police were called and Aunt Charlotte was arrested. She pleaded guilty and was placed on three years probation and fined $1,000.00. Aunt Bea complained that the use of an illegal drug meant that Aunt Charlotte win should be forfeited. The judges thought so but after research realized there was no violation of the rules and Aunt Charlotte remained the winner.

Virtually all of the consumers of the cupcakes declared they were the most awesome cupcakes ever. Over a dozen cupcakes were retained but strangely enough only one whole cupcake and one partially consumed cupcake were available by the time sentencing of Aunt Charlotte was scheduled. Since she pleaded guilty the whole cupcake was not placed in evidence but was enshrined in the county fair mini-museum. Aunt Charlotte to the chagrin of both aunts, Bea and Dorothy, became for a short period of time a media sensation.

As a result, the marriage of Angela and Karen received a great deal of attention. Karen was a paralegal, age 27, and Angela was a former beauty queen, was 26, and recent medical school graduate who intended to be a pediatrician.

ZUCCHINI

Their gay wedding received extensive media exposure. Some of the extended family who were vocal anti-gay marriage muted their comments and attended the wedding.

Aunts, Bea, Charlotte, and Dorothy did not attend the wedding or reception abiding by their largely religious view that gay marriage was a sin that could never be accepted. Angela and Karen were delighted that those three aunts did not mar their wedding.

Angela remarked "so much for zucchini and the county fair feud. Personally, I am never going to buy or eat zucchini". Karen said, "I will eat zucchini because I like the taste". Both Angela and Karen were too wise to let zucchini be of any consequence in their lives.

YIELD

Cathy, age 7, was playing with Trudy, Bob and Sam, likewise age 7, in the play ground 89 of their school at recess.

Sam had sand thrown at him by Cathy and he retaliated by grabbing her and holding her down. Sam told Cathy, "Yield. Say you are sorry." Cathy replied "Never will I yield." Bob pulled Sam off of Cathy.

From that day forward Cathy and Sam detested each other and often in school were in direct competition. In high school they both for three years were on the academic debate team. Invariably whatever side Cathy took Sam took the opposite and vice versa.

They were by far the best debaters on the team and for the first time ever the debate team was in the finals for the State. The teacher, Roger, talked to both Cathy and Sam and received from them they would put aside their profound dislike for each other and work sincerely as teammates and succeed for the debate team and their school. Each of them did put out their best effort. The debate team out of sixteen teams came out second in the State debate team championship. Cathy and Sam were excellent and worked very well together.

At the dinner honoring the debate team, Cathy stood up and after praising Sam for this efforts said "I will never yield to you." Sam made no response but to himself thought "Yes you will."

They each went to college and started their careers. They saw each other on occasions but did not socialize with each other. Twice they were in weddings for mutual friends. Cathy was a bridesmaid in one wedding and Sam knowing there would be friction declined to be a groomsman.

At that wedding, Sam asked Cathy to dance but Cathy said "Only if you will swear to never having any thought of my yielding to you." Sam spurned this and responded "Someday you will yield to me."

YIELD

In their senior year at college, they met at a debate competition where the question debated was "Can the equal rights amendment ever be in the U.S. Constitution?" Sam was on the team for his college, took the affirmative and Cathy for her college debate team was for the negative.

After their spirited persuasive debate, the judges declared a draw and neither team won or lost.

Both obtained LLB degrees and returned to their hometown and joined small law firms that specialized in litigation and trials. Over the next six years, Cathy and Sam often represented opposing litigants at trials. Both proved to be very skillful and soon were the go-to lawyers on many high profile civil cases. Rarely did they try a case to a conclusion and cases were settled.

At the Bar Association picnic, Sam wore a jersey with the work "Yield" and Cathy aware of this wore one stating in bright red "Never Yield".

When they were 31, they went to another city for a two day preliminary hearing to resolve pre-trial issues. They were always polite and civil in courtrooms to each other and did not show ever overt animosity. The law and their careers dominated their lives. They respected each as truly worthy legal adversaries.

During the first day, they engaged in serious settlement discussions. Cathy invited Sam to dinner to pursue this matter further.

During dinner they conversed about books, music and movies and enjoyed this discussion. In fact, they were very compatible and shared most values.

Before commencing the settlement negotiation, Cathy in all seriousness told Sam, "I have thought this for a long time that had the episode when we were seven never happened, we might have dated and who knows might be in a romantic relationship. I know it is 24 years too late but I am sorry I threw sand in your face. The only excuse or reason is that I liked you then and you ignored me and I wanted to get your attention. I am sorry."

YIELD

Sam responded, "I unconditionally accept your apology. I have often thought that I owe you an apology for my actions. I am sorry."

Both got up and hugged each other with ardor regardless of the presence of the other dinner patrons.

In the interest of compromise, they, unlike die hard politicians took the interests of their clients and in one hour settled the civil case.

The second day was canceled with the Court and they had a free day. Cathy and Sam decided to use that day to be together. They bowled; went sailing; played miniature golf; and ended that evening dancing together.

At five minutes before midnight, Cathy told Sam this by far had been the best day of her life. Sam said for him also.

They kissed and hugged and mutually decided to continue their romance. Cathy said "I yield" while Sam said "No need to ever yield".

Eight months later, Cathy and Sam had a legal marriage and both yielded from then on to each other.

X-RATED

Jonathan and Brandi had known each other since tenth grade. They dated for a few weeks in 12th grade but there was no spark. They went to the senior prom with other dates and did not dance together.

Each went to college and had careers, Jonathan being a radiologist and Brandi being a paralegal. They did return to their mid-sized city where they grew up.

They saw each other on occasion but no spark occurred with them.

Jonathan at age 26, married Sue, a registered nurse but they divorced in less than two years. Brandi tried a live-in relationship three times for several months at a time but each of these liaisons fizzled out.

Jonathan and Brandi each had a secret passion for X-rated movies and magazines. Neither had ever been into the active X-rated life and had no desire to do so.

Each did collect X-rated movies and enjoyed viewing them. It is possible that their sexual lives required this addiction to be able to function well. Neither ever revealed to friends, relatives or others this addiction.

In their city, in addition to online sources, there were two media stores that catered to and sold X-rated movies. Brandi was in one store having bought two new X-rated movies when Jonathan came in. Both felt some embarrassment but did converse in a friendly manner. Jonathan mentioned he had one of the movies and both eventually discussed these types of movies.

From one viewpoint, it was somewhat rare for a woman to be addicted to sexually explicit movies, or maybe not.

It was unusual for a woman to patronize these stores since most women had boyfriends or husbands who sought out such material or the same was bought on the internet.

X-RATED

Brandi invited Jonathan to a dinner date and he accepted. At that time, neither had an active dating relationship. They did have an interesting and stimulating dinner and brought each other current on their lives. For various reasons, neither discussed X-rated movies not said anything about their personal intimate lives.

They did talk about books and other matters. They had a lively though brief, part of the conversation about politics and for the first time discovered that Brandi was a "devout" democrat and Jonathan had always been a "dyed in the wool" republican. At the end of the spirited brief political remarks, they agreed not to have any argument about politics nor religion. Jonathan was a lapsed Catholic and Brandi for a long time was an agnostic but not an atheist.

They enjoyed this first real date so much they agreed to date exclusively.

On their third date, Jonathan came to the apartment of Brandi and they spent several hours viewing X-rated movies and enjoyed that activity. Thereafter, at least half of their dates were used to view each other's collections of X-rated movies and they thoroughly enjoyed the company of each other.

Brandi and Jonathan did marry and had three children. They had a good marriage and indulged in buying, collecting and viewing X-rated movies quietly and by and large secretly together.

WOMB

"Where am I? This place is warm and cozy. Why am I here? I can move but my arms do not do much but aha my legs are sturdy. I can kick my way out."

Susan turned to her husband, Ted and exclaimed, "The baby kicked me and here it comes again. I wonder what the baby is thinking."

"These walls are thick and tough and this is my prison. I want out into the sunshine and the world" in its' thin voice which did not project to any distance. He cried out, "Let me go-Let me free. Why cannot anyone hear me? I will try Morse code. Everyone knows that."

Susan said to Ted, "Now the baby is doing a rhythm as though trying to communicate." Ted replied, "The baby is kicking as all babies do in the seventh and eighth months. You know our child will not speak for a long time."

Susan kept thinking and also worrying. Susan requested a visit with her doctor and with Ted explained the eerie feeling she had that the baby was trying to communicate and she felt that the baby sensed something dangerous. The doctor said, "You are just entering the eighth month and it is normal to be anxious. Your due date is just 45 days away." Susan and Ted insisted and the doctor ordered immediate tests including a more intensive ultrasound. These tests were conducted promptly. An hour later, they were brought back to the doctor's office. The doctor, Janet, told them the tests showed a real problem and the only way to be sure is to at once be admitted to the hospital and have a Caesarian operation to deliver the baby at once. Susan and Ted agreed since this was the first baby for them and the first grandchild in both their families.

WOMB

Later that day, the baby was born. The baby, a boy, was healthy. The doctor said if Susan had not come in the baby would have died in a day or so in the womb. It was explained to Susan and Ted that something unknown was making the womb instead of being nurturing place a deadly place to keep the baby. This all turned out well. Due to this situation, doctors around the world were alerted to the toxic nature that some wombs could become and this explained several mysterious deaths of very healthy babies in the womb when the eighth month started.

The baby was named "Alert". Alert thought "It is a good thing I knew Morse code and could warn my parents about the danger of being in the womb."

VERGE

Ronald was taking a Sunday drive in his just purchased Lexus when he swerved to avoid hitting a doe. His vehicle swerved off the road and went down the slope on the right side but came to a stop when it went into a depression. Ronald who lived to study words and their meaning said to himself "Verge meaning to slope or sink. In avoiding the doe I did a double verge."

Ronald was not hurt much but his vehicle needed a tow. He tried from in the car to call out on his cell phone but had to get out to have decent service. He called AAA and was able to give them directions. His vehicle had GPS but not an "Onstar" device.

About two hours later a large tow truck arrived and the sign on its side read "McCory & daughter."

From the cab of the tow truck stepped Nanci, 26, who said she would bring the tow chain down the verge slope and attach it to Ronald's Lexus and pull him back on the road. It then can he established if the vehicle is operable.

Ronald who was 6 foot 3 inches tall and weighed 215 stared at Nanci, who was five foot five inches tall and might have weighed 120 pounds and who was dressed in heavy duty clothes and workmen boots and said, "Can you really do this? How experienced are you?" Nanci replied, "I will go on my way and you can try to get another tow truck with some big strong man to help you."

Ronald still dubious apologized. Nanci capably showed her talents and within twenty minutes had winched the Lexus up to the road. Although damaged the Lexus could be driven. As Nanci completed paperwork she lectured Ronald to obviously apply his brakes to slow down but never swerve to avoid hitting an animal. She quoted how many people were severely injured and died by swerving. Ronald meekly heard her out and drove away carefully.

Ronald was an attorney for an investment bank and was doing well financially and gaining daily experience and was on his way to be a success. Ronald was active socially.

VERGE

Ronald as he expressed, had a hole in his heart from three years ago when his mother, Alice, his sister, June, and his niece, Tammy, just two years of age, died in a car crash. Why their vehicle went off the road and swerved down a steep slope (another verge) and struck a mammoth oak tree was a mystery. It could be that an oncoming vehicle came into their lane and June, who was driving swerved or it was likely the swerve was to avoid a deer. In one event, Ronald lost his entire remaining immediate family and he still felt sorrow.

Ronald, over the next few days, constantly thought of perky Nanci. He learned that she was the only child of Tim, who operated a reputable and efficient auto repair shop and did tow jobs for AAA. Tim had a recent disabling injury so he could not drive the tow truck. Nanci, a 4-yr. college graduate had worked as a skilled auto mechanic for her father for years. Nanci had a studio where she did sculptures and worked about 24 hours a week for Tim. Nanci did the fine engine work and had an excellent reputation in that auto mechanic field. Nanci would do the occasional towing work for AAA.

Ronald sent Nanci three white roses and a handwritten note again apologizing and expressing his thanks for her help. Nanci was touched by this gesture and at the urging of Tim she called Ronald. That conversation led to a first date. At the dinner date, Ronald drew Nanci out about her dual skills, auto mechanic and sculptor. Ronald knew much about fine art since as a hobby he had for years practiced painting in oils. Ronald was passionate about legal matters and painting. Nanci and Ronald had an enjoyable dinner and proved to have compatible interests.

Neither of them had any serious previous romantic experience, although, they had dated before and neither was a virgin sexually.

VERGE

They took it slow and had the usual doubts about their unfolding love but about a year later did marry. Nanci needed to continue as a skilled auto mechanic. Tim had recovered so that Nanci rarely did AAA towing jobs but did one about six weeks after the marriage and towed out a new vehicle which had swerved down a slope (verge) and did lecture that driver as she had Ronald.

UNDERSTUDY

Throughout his life and he was the advanced age of 26, John always believed he was the understudy; the second stringer; the almost forgotten one.

In fact, in grade school due in part to a nervous stutter, John was rarely called upon in classrooms. John was a shy person and as a child effectively lived up to the adage: "Boys should be seen and not heard." John played the role of the" loner". In high school, John was one of the "others" not by being a cutup or a rebel without any cause but did not assert himself.

In his senior year, John went to a tryout for the school play and was picked to be the multiple understudy for several minor parts and on the last day of the play, John got on stage for less than two minutes doing a non-memorable walk and standing around part while uttering one word "WHY" which he shouted out rather than making "why" a sarcastic statement. This ended his stage "career" and he never tried out in college for a play.

In baseball and football, John was usually one of the last ones picked to play. John did make the school team in baseball at the practice level and was cut before the first regular game.

It is true that in 12 at bats, he hit once causing a double play. It is true that he committed several errors while fielding and throwing.

In tenth grade he went out for football and was assigned to be a guard but at 115 pounds, he, despite a desire to play and willing to be hurt was released from the football team. John enjoyed running but proved to be too slow in track and cross country. John was good at science classes and excelled in Math and History. John went to college and had a half-tuition scholarship so that in academic endeavors John was not an understudy.

UNDERSTUDY

John liked girls and young women but was very shy and a devout introvert. John did get up the courage to ask Betty, a rather plain looking girl to the senior prom but a day before Betty said she was going to the prom with another and John did not attend any school prom or dances. John secretly had taken dance lessons and was a "good" dancer.

John did not make any effort to date until during his second year in law school.

John had a scholarship covering tuition and books at law school. John had worked since he was fourteen at various jobs and had sufficient funds so he did not have student loans and in fact had about $1,000.00 upon graduation from law school.

John admired Emily, a fellow law student for her tenacity in class and her intelligence. John, who was a trim 165 pounds, was 5 foot ten; had wavy brown hair; and hazel eyes was moderately attractive. Emily was a knockout having ash blond hair and green eyes, and was 5 foot six inches and weighed about 120 pounds. Emily was seemingly an extrovert and was both witty and friendly. John and Emily opposed each other in a mock appellate court trial and John won the legal match. Before the scheduled argument, John gave Emily hand-painted picture and Emily gave John a delicious cake. The day after the mock trial, John asked Emily to go on a date for dinner but Emily declined telling John she had decided to leave law school to be a num. Emily told John if she was inclined to date she would have been happy to date John but she accepted her higher purpose and calling.

John accepted this result, wishing Emily well, and thought to himself "once an understudy, always so. I am a loser and a loner and will be forever."

UNDERSTUDY

John joined a small law firm and succeeded in being a very able lawyer. A fellow associate, Judith, a year older than John was a small law firm and succeeded in being a very able lawyer. A fellow associate, Judith, year older than John was asked to be a mentor to John so he could readily know the more practical aspects and procedures of being an attorney with this law firm.

Judith was attractive and focused on John as a man and not just a fellow attorney. Judith saw in John someone she could admire and respect and believed he could be the one for her in her desire to be married and to have a family. Judith over time fully overcame John's shyness. John did commence his journey to cease being an understudy and move to being a mature person. For two years, Judith did whatever was needed to help John to realize his potential.

Judith finally proposed to John and to his credit John said yes at once. They did marry and before Judith died, they had celebrated over 50 years together. They had four children, 8 grandchildren and 9 great grandchildren. By all measures they had a good life together.

John always remembered what Judith said to him after they on their honeymoon had several times consummated their marriage. "John, you are no longer an understudy".

TEPID

Marcia was a woman in her late twenties who was in effect a moderate in all things. Marcia considered herself a conservative in dress and makeup; average in looks; not a hot item nor a cold one so far as romance and sexuality were involved. Marcia had little interest in political matters. She avoided confrontation. The best example Marcia had that she did not like her shower cold nor hot but medium warm or tepid. Marcia when thinking about herself thought of herself as tepid. Marcia was 5 foot 5 inches tall; weight between 130 and 140; she had bland dull chestnut hair. Her eyes were brown and rarely sparkled; she had a fair complexion with some freckles. Marcia when in a happy state did have a warm (much more than tepid) engaging inviting smile. Marcia was well educated having a BA in economics and for the last four years was an assistant in the economics department of the college.

Marcia did have a sporadic dating situation. Her only attempt to have a live in relationship lasted a few months and the breakup was not traumatic but just oozed away until the end; a handshake upon parting. Marcia's sex life was dull since it was based mostly on a desire to be "normal" for her age and time and had no spark of any kind. Marcia did like children and sometimes "babysat" her brother's children, Sandy an adorable three year old, and Steve, an energetic four plus.

Marcia occasionally gave some thoughts to her situation and she wisely did not want to marry just to be married. Marcia believed in the concept of love but had never felt it nor experienced love first hand.

Some years before Marcia had tentatively tried to have a lesbian affair but came to naught since she had no possible sexual feelings for women. Marcia did have a group of friends but over time these friendships were withering away since they moved away for careers or marriage.

TEPID

Marcia had two-week vacation time and on the spur of the moment decided to go to a spa resort for one of those weeks. Although quite expensive Marcia thought the change would be good for her.

Marcia did go to the spa and learned how better to enhance her looks, learning about hair styling; better use of makeup; and how to exercise more efficiently. Marcia shed four pounds while at the Spa.

For the second week Marcia as a dare to herself, went on an adventure trip which involved rock climbing, hiking and intensive exercise.

Marcia came back from her vacation with a new hairdo with highlights, a subdued but better makeup which emphasized her smile; a somewhat toned but tired body; and for the first time in many years, weighed under 130 years.

Marcia in her teen years had enjoyed bowling and had some skill in bowling. Upon her return, Marcia signed up for two bowling leagues; purchased needed equipment and several times a week practiced bowling before the leagues started. In a short time Marcia met other bowlers and practiced often. As a result Marcia was averaging over 180 and felt like a new person. Marcia soon had several bowling friends and when leagues started Marcia was more than comfortable. These leagues were for good bowlers who wanted to be intensely competitive but were not the elite bowling leagues for the highly skilled. One league was composed of teams of women and during that season Marcia proved herself to be one of the better bowlers, attaining an average of 187; bowling a high game of 257 and three game series of 713.

The other league was a mixed league of men and women. Marcia had been assigned to a team where one couple was married and the others were in a committed relationship. Marcia took the position she was there to be with other bowlers and to do her best at bowling. Marcia succeeded having an average of 192, bowling a game of 266 and 3-game series of 744.

TEPID

Marcia had found something to do where she could achieve something which would last and give her inner pride.

Marcia, due in part to her enhanced attractive looks and her more athletic body, but due more to quit being tepid in self-esteem and personality was dating more. Marcia found she attracted more men to date (although during the bowling year there were only four) and believed in herself so that she knew that romance and marriage and a family would come in time.

Marcia knew that becoming warm or hot and no longer tepid was the perceived secret for her. And so it was.

SHREW

Kate when she was 8 years old saw the movie "Taming of the Shrew" and a few days later read the play by Shakespeare bearing the same title. Kate at that early age decided she was going to be a smart shrew believing that is a sure method to find a man to marry and be happy with.

At school, Kate acted as the witty one being sarcastic often and making rather cruel cutting remarks. Kate got the well deserved reputation of being prickly and independent. Kate always turned a boy's compliment into a sarcastic and cutting remark. A few girls became her friend in school since they saw Kate as a free spirit, who spoke her mind regardless of consequences. Kate did very well academically and was third in her large senior class.

In 11th grade the school put on a condensed version of the play. Many thought that Kate should play Katherine, the shrew, but Kate chose to play Bianca, the outwardly demure and polite woman but who in reality was a true shrew.

In the play, although the leads were Katherine and Petrucio, when Kate as Bianca was on the stage, she dominated the stage and enthralled the audience.

Throughout school, Kate never met a young man who she thought was remotely worthy of her and used her acerbic sharp shrewish tongue to put them down. Kate felt good at her method of dominating these young men but as a result she had few dates and no real romance. Kate's reputation as a shrew grew so that even though she was very attractive and certainly threw off an aura of sexuality, no young man wanted to take a chance on taming Kate.

Kate actually did not need a man to tame her but did want and need a man to fulfill her. Kate believed that she had a lot to offer any man willing to woo her. As said, she was attractive, had a deep sexual nature; was intelligent and well-educated; aimed for a career after college as a dedicated biologist; was very sensible with regard to money; was athletic having played tennis and volleyball on high school teams to justified acclaim. Of course, Kate had a more than sharp tongue and was a shrew.

SHREW

When Kate arrived at college, she tried to change and to be less sharp tongued. However, she often let her words and remarks escape before pausing and thinking so she soon alienated fellow students. Kate did make the college teams in both volleyball and tennis and did very well during the four years in college. Kate was a superb student and most of the instructors and professors accepted the shrewish ways of Kate and objectively taught her as an intelligent would be biologist. Kate did date during college but failed to find the one. One student, a senior, showed real interest in Kate and she responded for a record five weeks till they started to argue about religious differences which proved too much for any continuing relationship. During those five weeks Kate was far less shrewish and found real enjoyment in intelligent conversation. Kate felt no true need to be a shrew to Kenneth because she discovered the joy of not being a shrew with someone she cared for and admired. Other than the religious profound difference which doomed their future, Kate and Kenneth found many shared values and areas where they were compatible. They did not always agree but more often than not could discuss matters without getting angry and nasty.

Kate learned from that period of time that there was hope for her. Kate did secure a Master's degree in biology.

Kate was recruited and did accept employment with a relatively new Biology firm and did very well in her chosen profession

Kate throughout her life did remain a sharp tongued woman and to some continued to be a shrew but learned over time to give some thought usually before making a sarcastic or shrewish statement and by and large curbed her shrewish personality.

Kate at a whim attended her 10-yr. high school reunion and discovered that her reputation as a shrew was still present but more accepted. During that evening by taming her shrewish disposition, many accepted her the way she was.

SHREW

One young man who never approached Kate in high school introduced himself to her by saying "My name is Keith and I am certain you do not remember me. I was scared to even talk to you in high school but I have worked for years on changing my extreme shyness personality. This coming up to you is another step on my journey to change." Kate responded by saying ,"If I can truly change from being a shrew, you can overcome shyness by showing your true self and gaining self-confidence. If you want to take a chance on me and I will do likewise. Please accept this as I intend it and have dinner with me tomorrow night."

Keith said yes and they had an enjoyable dinner. They laughed at quips and stories. They did converse in a way that gave each other some hope that not only were they "compatible" but that something good for both of them might happen. This was far from a "love at first sight" situation but they both saw in the other a somewhat damaged soul and that they might help each other. Keith and Kate did date but not exclusively for about one year. They had no serious disagreements. They did not suddenly find love together but Keith made serious efforts to overcome his shyness and basically succeeded.

Kate never overcame her shrewish disposition but did moderate it to better than tolerable limits.

Was it possible that Kate did follow the movie and play so that she as a shrew was tamed? Kate would say yes as would Keith did when they celebrated their third wedding anniversary welcoming with joy their daughter, Crystal, born on their anniversary.

RELEASE

Joseph spent the year he was seventeen in a juvenile detention facility for a crime he did not commit. Often an adult is freed on the basis that his conviction was illegal and that is duly noted in the media.

Joseph's release was not so noted. Sometimes adults are compensated by a money award for false imprisonment but not Joseph. Joseph would have remained in the juvenile prison until his release when he reached age 21 if the two Court of Common Pleas judges had not been discovered criminally selling juveniles to the prison for money and gifts. There were over 600 juveniles released on the basis of false imprisonment.

Joseph returned to live with his parents while he attended his senior year in school. Some law firms seeing an opportunity approached Joseph to urge him to file a lawsuit but Joseph refused. Joseph quietly completed his senior year. Since Joseph was 6 foot 2 inches tall and weighed 195 pounds and was well conditioned fellow students did not bother Joseph. He was an end on the football team and forward on the basketball team. Joseph also resumed his golfing endeavor and came in fourth in the State Championship.

Joseph received a scholarship to college based on his athletic abilities and his academic record. He was a stellar student and athlete. During his second year he wrote under an assumed name a harrowing fictionalized novel about life in a juvenile detention facility and this novel was a best seller and was optioned for a TV movie (which was never produced). Joseph earned enough from this novel so that he had zero student loans and had some funds after graduation.

Joseph decided to move to Chicago and secured employment with a start-up company which was well-financed. Joseph, since his major was chemistry, had a job in the lab and earned about $15.00 per hour as his starting wage. Joseph did continue to write but did not seek publication. He stayed with the firm and was promoted so that by the time he was 29 he was the chief chemist.

RELEASE

Joseph after moving to Chicago did have dates but found that many of the young women were too shallow since they had no interest in political and national matters and each of these short time relationships terminated.

Joseph did meet Janet, who was 28, and a paralegal and they commenced exclusive dating. Some three months later, Joseph thought that Janet was the one he sought and told her about his false imprisonment and release. Janet was silent and Joseph thought she was turned off by this revelation. That was not true and Janet slowly told Joseph she was also similarly falsely imprisoned but for over two years. Janet told Joseph their relationship would be doomed since they both carried the scars of their background. Joseph realized that Janet was right and accepted their breakup. Janet urged Joseph to keep the previously planned family dinner with her family and he did so.

At that delightful Sunday dinner, Joseph met Janet's younger sister, Alicia, 26, who was also a paralegal. Joseph to his wonderment fell in love with Alicia and she did likewise. Love-true love-at first sight seems fiction but of course, Joseph and Alicia spent several hours together although always in the company of Janet, her parents Sid and May and her brother Robert. However, Joseph and Alicia gravitated to one another and to say the least sparks flew between them.

Within ten days, Joseph proposed and Alicia said yes. In just less than ninety days, they were married. Joseph revealed his false imprisonment and release to Alicia before their first date. Alicia simple response was "I caught you after your release and you shall ever be mine."

Janet, a year later, married Howard an attorney and they stayed close to Joseph and Alicia and each of their families enjoyed numerous happy occasions together.

RELEASE

Throughout their life together and it was very long and filled with ecstasy and surprises and blessed with three children and seven grandchildren. Joseph and Alicia constantly discovered to their endless delight that their love for each other grew.

QUEST

Raymond on his fifth birthday received a picture book about King Arthur and the Knights of the Round Table. Raymond was enthralled at the colors, the glamour, and the swordfights. He was in rapture concerning the noble quests that the knights embarked on regardless of the danger involved. Whether the quest was to find a chalice, or a gem or a scroll; or to rescue a lady; or restore a lord to his castle, Raymond pictured himself doing this type of quest. Raymond throughout his childhood had repeated dreams, both at night and daydreams, where he was the hero in these quests.

As time went on Raymond obtained several books about King Arthur, Merlin, Sir Lancelot, Guinevere, the Lady of the Lake, Sir Gawain, and the vast number of knights, etc.

Raymond studied that era of British history. He excelled in History and Geography in High School and majored in History and Medieval Era in college. One of his prized possessions was a chess set with medieval figurines. He played chess but was so inept that he lost repeatedly, not on purpose, to his nephew, Trent, who was seven and a mediocre chess player. Raymond did enter a local round robin chess tournament and lost to every participant so fast that speed dating would seem to be a slow journey.

Raymond did seek quests during his life. When he was six he rescued another boy at the sandbox by standing up to two bullying brothers and only had a cut lip and twisted fingers to show for it. The rescued boy two days later was actively playing with the two brothers.

QUEST

When Raymond was nine, he got in trouble since he insisted on taking a lady across a street she did not want to cross. Until Raymond was entering college it seemed his endless quest to be good if not perfect at quests was doomed. Every effort by Raymond was a failure and caused him no end of difficulty. (Readers if any and if interested there is a book setting forth in exquisite detail many but not all of the guests of Raymond from age 5 to age eighteen- fateful 13 number. It is out of print having sold 37 copies out of run of 1500. It's title was "The Endless Quest by a Naïve Male Person of Successful Quests hampered by family, the public, and non-knowing others and all those who detested Medieval times and Quests.)

Starting in college and in his working life as a junior historian specializing in Medieval Times at the museum, Raymond took a more mature view regarding quests. Such a quest had to have a detailed plan; have a clear attainable objective; pass a cost benefit analysis. Finally such quest had to pass his meditation test which sometimes lasted several minutes to days.

Skipping over all but one quest (the quests are a sequel book which sold exactly 34 copies) the following was the essential quest of Raymond's life.

At age 29, Raymond decided to perform a permanent personal quest to find a woman to marry and to have a family. Raymond selected three fellow employees to pursue for this marriage quest. Amy was not the one since she was secretly married for two weeks and still happy. Brenda was out after one date since she casually mentioned that she had recently broke up a committed relationship of four years with her dear friend Alice.

Since Raymond had a firm desire virtually obsessive to fulfill his marriage quest he began a dedicated romance with Clarice, who was 28, a fellow historian at work whose specialty was the history of the Spanish-American war and its impact on modern life.

QUEST

Clarice and Raymond clicked and this quest ended in a marriage at the Museum. They decided to have the wedding and reception with all guests dressed in period costumes. Raymond, the groom, dressed as Sir Gay and Clarice was beautifully dressed In a Victorian wedding dress.

Raymond believed in quests and knew he had achieved the best quest and was finally a success at a quest by deciding to go ahead with the marriage quest and winning the love of Clarice.

Raymond wished everyone would have a quest.

PASTEL

Irene, an amateur painter of some note, always stated that bright colors hurt her vision and therefore she only used pastel and even then the palest of shades. It was often said that Irene could have had a brilliant career as a painter if she would have moved on from pastels to bright hues. Irene who had a career as an actuary with an insurance firm always responded that she was happy the way she was and had no desire to change.

Irene, who went to Museums and art shows, always carried in her purse sunglasses to shield her eyes if bright colored painting or art work was present.

Irene had her modern apartment decorated in muted pastel colors; had neutral or pastel colors regarding furniture; had paintings and artwork only in pastel shades. When invited to visit others she usually asked what the décor was in their homes and rarely visited anyone utilizing bright colors. Irene only patronized restaurants using muted pastels for their décor. Irene had no friends who dressed in bright hues. At her employment she chose pastel colors to the extent possible and only if absolutely required would enter the offices of fellow employees who had chosen bright colors.

Irene did have a serious eyesight problem which in fact impaired her vision if she saw bright colors. There was no cure or treatment for this rare disorder. Irene was advised to avoid as much as possible being where bright colors pre-dominated.

PASTEL

Irene had always since early childhood questioned her sexual orientation. She forced herself in denying this matter to go no dates with men. Whenever even a kiss or hug occurred, her vision only saw bright colors and she actually became violently ill. After a few such episodes, Irene knew she was a lesbian and sought out other women. Irene for years had avoided coming out of the closet but finally decided for her mental health she should become more public with her needed sexual preferences. Irene did tell her close relatives and some fellow employees. Irene's work as an n insurance actuary was exceptional and she was not harassed at work.

Irene fell in love with Sybil, a year younger than Irene. Sybil was an actress of some note and had announced her lesbianism when she was fourteen years old and had always been quite open about this matter. Irene and Sybil were truly compatible with regards to values; interests; and in every meaningful way except for one. Sybil only liked bright colors and detested all pastel shades. Sybil had no rare vision problem but hated all pastel shades in every manner, and became ill if she saw or was in the presence of pastels.

The evening they met, Irene and Sybil talked for over four hours and fell in love. About ten minutes before the end Sybil told Irene of her abhorrence of pastels and Irene responded saying she had a vision disorder regarding bright colors.

Both Irena and Sybil knew this was a deal breaker and they parted in bitter sorrow and never saw each other again.

It has been said that color has no impact but a great love ended via pastels and bright colors.

CLOUD

Arnold worked at a pharmacy and was 28 years old. Arnold had passion for going out usually on Sunday afternoons laying on a blanket and dozing while watching clouds in the sky. Sometimes Arnold fell asleep and the clouds would form nightmare images such as vicious fighting and dying. Arnold thought that the clouds were warring on each other. He often woke up and felt despair.

The best times for Arnold which were more often was just the playful antics of the clouds meeting and merging together. Sometimes the clouds would have brilliant light streaks and would appear as cloud rainbows.

Arnold got into the habit of having a day dream which then became more real when he saw clouds act the way he dreamed. By far his favorite cloud dream was when he saw a cloud turn into himself as he imagined it and then his cloud met a lovely cloud he named Patricia, which was followed by three smaller clouds who he did not name but perceived as the three children of himself and Patricia.

One day, Arnold noticed a new store had opened and he was struck by its name "Cloud". He went in the store on opening day and found it was a niche store with knickknacks; tourist items; and a soda fountain. A young woman was at the soda fountain and her name tag read "Patricia".

Arnold conversed with Patricia and discovered she worked there on a part-time basis while completing her last year at college. Patricia was 25 years old and explained she had to take two years off because her father needed her at home before he died. She liked this new store "Cloud" and was in a small way a partial owner.

Patricia told Arnold a few days later when they went to see a movie and were having a late snack that she was to receive her Master's degree in a few months in psychology and most likely had a position waiting for her so she could live in this city.

CLOUD

Arnold related to Patricia his hobby of viewing clouds and Patricia said she used to go with her Dad when he was well and watch not just clouds but the nearby lake and sail boats.

The very next Sunday, Arnold and Patricia spent Sunday afternoon lounging and watching the intricate patterns of the clouds. Patricia remarked about two good sized clouds followed by three smaller ones and said it was her dream to be married, like her parents had and that three children would be ideal.

Arnold promptly told Patricia about his day dream and his constant vision of the five cloud formation.

For the next six months during which Patricia graduated and started her career, they were a constant couple and dated regularly. On a day that started out cloudless, as Arnold asked Patricia to marry him in front of the "cloud" store she said "sure" and as that word was uttered clouds came into the sky.

They were married and did have within six years, three children. Arnold in a playful mood wanted to name them "Cloudy" "Cloudier" and "Cloudiest" but reason prevailed. Their names were Tricia; Ronald; and Lacey.

The best times they had as a family was going on most Sundays and having a picnic and watched the ever changing patterns of the clouds. The children never tired of hearing how Arnold and Patricia met; the store which still existed called "cloud" and the marriage proposal; and especially the story of clouds and dreams which came true.

VIOLIN

Joseph, a 27 year old computer analyst; was doing what he did best; lounging near the famous Academy for Music to see which young female he could meet. Joseph played several musical instruments but was not proficient in any. He often referred to himself as a "Joseph of all musical trades and the master of none."

Joseph was good looking, and had a ready patter of talk about music. He rarely read a book but did study through the internet glib remarks regarding piano, trombone, saxophone, flute, cello and violin. He could carry on a conversation sounding like he knew something but if he was talking to someone who studies music he turned to his charm and wit.

Joseph had just broken up with Sally, a flutist, a week before and was on the lookout for actually a violinist. He figured he could talk about the durable strings, the curve of the wood, etc. to initially make progress..

Joseph had seen Uranus, a violinist, whom he had learned had recently moved for her first position with the orchestra as second violinist. Joseph was easy to talk to and had several acquaintances in the local music scene.

When one day Uranus approached, a heavy set man accosted her and grabbed the violin case and ran towards where Joseph was waiting. Joseph, not wanting to injure his hands, deftly tripped the thief, and recovered the violin case and ran to Uranus and gave it to her while the thief limped away.

Joseph, thinking he would act smart, told Uranus, "Fair lady, from Joseph, your knight, I return your Strad violin intact". Uranus who indeed was fair of complexion, replied that this was good violin but not a Strad.

Uranus carefully opened the case and tucked the violin under her dainty chin and drew the bow across and said "there is no damage-it still plays well-by the way, many thanks."

Joseph took the bow and violin and commenced to play it. Joseph with a catch in his voice pronounced that all was well and remarked how good the pitch and timbre was with regard to the violin.

VIOLIN

Joseph asked Uranus to have dinner with him that evening and she without hesitating, agreed.

Joseph promptly made a reservation at a Romanian restaurant where the food was inexpensive but they had a trio of strolling violinists who played either sorrowful music or catchy dancing tunes.

Uranus was enthralled by Joseph and soon they were a couple. Uranus knew that Joseph did know some matters concerning music and instruments but displayed his lack of education in his remarks and he was less than mediocre when he tried to play any and all musical instruments.

Uranus was clear eyed 23 years old and was going to be a superb violin soloist. As time went on Joseph wanted Uranus to practice less and be with him more. Uranus, who had found her passion when she was five and her father Fred spent countless hours with her showing her in his limited way how to play the violin, desired to live her passion.

Fred, father of Uranus, died when she was thirteen but did live and long enough to know that Uranus would be a great violinist and would for sure far surpass Fred.

At many events, Uranus and Fred played violin duets to great applause.

When Fred was dying, Uranus played every evening solo renditions on the violin for him and she promised that her passion for the violin would never wane.

Uranus promised herself that the priority for her life was to be herself; to play beauty in music; and to fulfill her dream and that of her father that she achieve a memorable lasting violinist career.

Uranus told Joseph all this and told him that although he was witty and charming that they were actually on different paths.

Uranus received within days an offer to be first soloist violinist with the London Symphony and had a record contract with a music company re: playing the violin with the offer of touring as a featured violin soloists and she accepted this.

VIOLIN

Uranus went on the achieve greatness in Music. Joseph came to accept that his shallow attitude towards women and dating would only lead him to disaster and he changed his ways and be became a serious acting and talking person.

Uranus, had a very good recording and touring career, and did marry by sheer coincidence, Fred, also a violinist. They had three children and often lovely violin duet music would fill the evening.

CLOWN MAJESTIC

Roy had been a clown for over thirteen years. Roy had a serious problem since he was an inept clown but his ineptness rarely brought laughter to the people specifically children seeing him at the circus. Most times people laughed at him and not with him. Typical remarks were: "Where did you go to clown school – in Russia? My three year old is a better clown than you are. Can't you even fake it to act funny?"

Roy was at the lowest ebb of his life since all he ever wanted was to make people and children laugh. The other clowns were avoiding him and some openly wanted him to leave.

Roy talked to June, the fat lady, and one of his few friends and said why is there not a rehab place for clowns to go to learn to be clowns and funny and to have self-confidence. Roy was told why did he not start such a rehab school but his self-esteem was so poor he could not even conceive of being part of such an adventure.

Three unrelated things happened to Roy. He had a dream in multi-color which showed Roy as a young clown and the sky was dazzling and in brilliant hues the clouds changed to letters that spelled out "majestic". The next day Roy visited the fortune teller and in a few minutes she intoned in a quiet surreal way the word "majestic". Roy did his clown routine to a sparse audience early afternoon and stared at two children who had a sign that read "majestic".

Roy thought about that word "majestic" for his mental span of four and a half minutes and took this as an omen. Roy had the word "majestic" sewn on each of his clown costumes and started to proclaim himself as "Majestic" the clown.

Very soon, Roy became known as the clown Majestic; his self-esteem and confidence soared and he became the favored clown of the circus. He became so proud he had his name legally changed to Majestic and he finally had the courage to propose to Rosie, the trapeze artist. They were married and each of their five children were named Majestic. Roy always thought "what one word could do".

FAMILY

Jenny, age 30, after eight months of serious dating, married Ralph, ten years older. Ralph had been married to Julie who left when their two boys, Jim and Jon, were 6 and 4 years old. Jim was now 11 and Jon was almost 9 when the new marriage occurred. Jenny did connect with Jim during the months of courtship but Jon showed his resentment for Jenny.

Julie had never returned and played no part in the lives of the boys except that Jon seemingly always would remember an angel in white tucking him at night and giving him a fierce hug and would kiss him several times from his brow and ears and always end with a soft moist kiss on his lips. To Jon, that angel was his real mother, Julie.

Jenny prepared home cooked meals which had been lacking in the five years that Ralph had been in the role of a single father. But Jon would make constant and cruel remarks about the meals Jenny would hold back tears. Nothing Jenny did was of any effect on Jon. Every day was a testing time for all of them.

Jenny for seven years had been a paralegal with a three person law firm and truly loved her career. She had a dream of actually going to law school and being a lawyer.

Jenny wanted this marriage to Ralph to work and she recalled her one year marriage when she was 22 and which ended with bitterness because her then husband, Dave, made it clear after they were married that he never wanted children, shattering Jenny's desire to have a real family.

About two months after the wedding, Jenny told Ralph she wanted at least two children so that there would be a robust family but that she has given up on Jon and could not conceive that he would ever accept Jenny as part of the family. Jenny said she would wait one more month and then she would leave.

FAMILY

Ralph had tried repeatedly to talk to and with Jon but to no avail — Jon had an unrealistic dreamlike love for Julie and resented Jenny making any effort to be his mother. Jenny had told Ralph that he should not punish Jon in any manner. For the next month Jenny made every effort to please Jon and to show him real affection but could be nothing to convince Jon to merge his feelings so that they would be a family.

Jim, the older son, came to adore Jenny and wanted the marriage to be happy but realized that the adverse attitude of Jon was going to shatter forever the family.

A few days before the month was up, Jim became very ill and was taken to the hospital. It developed that Jim had a blood disorder and needed a rare type of bone marrow transplant to survive. Jon did love his brother Jim and visited him in the hospital. Jim had urged Jon to give up his Julie fantasy but Jon clung to this. Time was running out for him and he was growing weaker by the day. Jenny asked the doctors to test her blood and it was found that Jenny could donate bone marrow to save the life of Jim and she did so. Jim survived and came home the same day Jenny was to move out. Despite the pleas of both Ralph and Jim, Jenny left.

For the next week or so Jon put on a false face of elation since with Jenny gone and he had Ralph and Jim all to himself and he could cling to the dream of Julie.

Jon finally noticed that there was deep gloom with Jenny gone. Everyone displayed unhappiness and moped around. Jon had secretly kept a "diary" sporadically written by Julie and Jon in his hurt feelings went to his room and for the first time opened the "diary" and read Julie's writing days before her departure where she wrote: "I will be so happy to again see Dick and no longer have the nerdy brats around. I particularly detest Jon and his clinging ways and I will be so happy to never see him again. Freedom at last for me."

It took Jon a while to have those words of Julie sink in and Jon then realized how wrong he was and how badly he acted towards Jenny.

FAMILY

Jon took the bus and went to the building where Jenny worked. It was noontime and Jon found Jenny. Jon told Jenny his tale of woe and how sorry he was and put stress on the despair shown by Ralph and Jim and now himself.

Jon mentioned to Jenny that she was always telling a story that if one is really sorry and wants a family that a second chance or more will be provided to make happiness occur. Jenny recalled her favorite uncle, Max, had always taught her the truism "You must suffer sorrow to find family happiness and give freely second chances".

Jenny gave Jon a big hug and said she would give the family a second chance and said Jon could plan the surprise return of Jenny the next evening at precisely six p.m.

Jon returned home and kept this secret. Jon did not destroy the several pictures he had of Julie but put them away in his closet. Jon made a solemn vow to himself that he would for the rest of his life find the way to care for and to love Jenny.

When Jenny walked in the door, Jon expressed his new found true feelings by telling Jenny while hugging her that he loved her, would treat her and consider Jenny his bona fide mother and never disrespect her again.

Ralph and Jim did likewise and Jenny resumed her place with her family.

BLISS

Ruth and Rodger were married for two years plus when Ruth finally realized they had fallen into the trap each of their parents had been in seemingly always.

Ruth exclaimed "We are using the blame game. Every time we discuss anything we each blame the other and constantly reiterated past grievances. It is never our personal fault and responsibility but I lay the blame on you and you do likewise." Rodger also seeing this truth, agreed.

Both Ruth and Roger and their friends, relatives, co-workers and others all believed that their marriage was blessed and that they lived in "bliss."

Their mutual good friend, Holly, had told them they were living in a dream "bliss" world and that reality will happen. Ruth and Rodger had wanted children but had no success. In fact, Ruth had two miscarriages, each when she was pregnant for about two months. They each had good careers and were contemplating going for fertility tests and procedures. They were in their mid-twenties and did not want to consider adoption and neither wanted to consider surrogacy birth. Each had several nieces and nephews and enjoyed being with children.

One evening, Ruth was reading a magazine and saw an article regarding rehab specially for couples who were enmeshed in the "blame game" whether this "game was with each other or regarding other family members, friends or relating to employment." They decided to both take vacation time and spend a week at this rehab facility.

They did go and spent a "vacation" in the spa atmosphere of this "Blame" rehab center.

They learned that the "bliss" marriage was a façade and each had married the other to escape from the blame game they endured with their families. Ruth and Rodger came to the realization that they could cease in large measure blaming others for their troubles and learned to take personal responsibility for themselves. They knew this specialized "blame' rehab center was beneficial to each of them.

BLISS

They talked to their very good friend, Holly, and said they were going to get a divorce. They did so and remained friends. Both Ruth and Rodger found out that they needed to seek lasting relationship with someone else and to refrain as much as possible from blaming others. Their "bliss' marriage had never really existed and did end.

WORD

Jeremy, 43 years old, was a successful accountant. Jeremy was a confirmed bachelor and rarely dated. Over the last 14 years, Jeremy had three books published.

One was a semi-memoir which was panned by the four critics who reviewed it as a banal-trite and "as interesting as dirty dishwater"

Despite this failure Jeremy had a second non-best seller published which was a thinly veiled sarcastic story of well-known celebrities. There were 247 copies sold. A different publisher about four years previous published a mystery novel penned by Jeremy. The best critic review stated "Must read pages 111 and 147 and do not miss page 232. They show promise but the remaining 322 pages need not be read." Other reviews were less positive. Strangely enough this book had 1,645 book sales.

Jeremy did believe in himself and thought of himself as an author, which in fact he was, with triple failures.

Jeremy musing on his wordsmith or as a writer of words talked to his best friend, John, about an episode twelve years before.

A little child was lost in the woods and Jeremy volunteered to be in one of the search parties. Jeremy did not find the child but was always proud that he participated for three days. It was a mystery whether the child was lost or if someone had taken the child and left the child to die. No charges were ever filed but rumors flew.

John told Jeremy that he should write that tale as his fourth book and stated that the publisher would accept that book from Jeremy. Jeremy did talk to the editor and received approval to go forward.

Jeremy spent two months reading newspaper stories about the "lost child" and interviewed several people.

Jeremy did not know if he should write this as fiction; or as a story based on a true event; or as a non-fiction true book.

WORD

Since Jeremy could not decide and his best friend, John, would not decide for him, Jeremy decided to write three books using those three concepts.

Within three months, Jeremy had lost all focus and found he was in a quicksand of words. Jeremy started to have dreams/nightmares where words leapt over sheep; comingled as clouds of words; became dazzling in brilliant merging colors. John, when asked by Jeremy, told him he was the wordsmith; the master of words; that he should think of words as his friends and tools and start to use words in proper ways.

Jeremy had a brilliant idea and used his mastery of words and produced a book, which did become a best seller, by merging with imagination all three concepts into one book.

Jeremy finally discovered what "word" was.

COUCH

The paisley covered couch was acquired about ten years ago by the Winslow's, Amy and Jerry. They had a large home and when viewed in the showroom, Amy liked this couch. But when placed in their living room, the couch, well constructed, and reasonably comfortable, did not quite fit the décor. Within a week, the couch was banished to the attached apartment used for guests. No one who occupied that area ever complained.

Jerry's elderly uncle, Raymond, fell on hard times and came to live with the Winslow's' for a few years. Raymond made it a point to state how he liked the paisley couch and when he moved he was allowed to take it with him.

Raymond died and rather than selling the couch, his heirs and executor donated the paisley couch and some other furniture to a charity.

One day, Cheryl and Ted, married a few months came to the charity outlet. Cheryl saw the paisley couch and knew it would suit them as newlyweds. They paid $25.00 for the couch and asked their friend, Sam, if they could borrow his pickup truck to take it home to their one -bedroom apartment. Sam, always willing to help, drove his truck with the paisley couch and it was soon the prime piece of furniture in their otherwise sparse living room. For two months, Cheryl and Ted sat on the couch watching TV and Netflix movies.

Cheryl was four months pregnant with their first child when Ted was laid off from his employment. Since Ted was considered an independent contractor he could not apply for unemployment compensation. During the next month, Cheryl and Ted applied for food assistance and pending was their application for welfare and rent assistance. Cheryl did have a father who had recently married but he gave them some money. Ted was estranged from his parents and they rendered no help. Sam, their good friend, found some odd jobs for Ted.

COUCH

One evening, Ted noticed that the couch was wobbly. Cheryl and Ted turned the couch over and Cheryl discovered a package in the bottom of the couch. It was a heavy manila envelope and on the front in cursive writing stated, "Whoever finds this shall own it since I have died and have no need. It is my sincere wish that the finder really has a need for this gift".

They carefully opened the package and found twenties, tens, fifties and several hundreds. Adding them there was $13,260.00.

Cheryl and Ted tried to find out who had left the package to no avail. Ted used some of these funds to go to technical school and did find a well paying job. Cheryl used some for the needs of their first child.

They kept the paisley couch and maintained it for the rest of their lives.

CLEAN MOUSE

A young mouse always thought his name was "eek" because everyone seemingly who saw him yelled "eek!"

The mouse lived as most mice did in filth and squalor. The neighbors were rats and rats spelled danger.

Eek saw himself in a cracked mirror one day and liked not what he saw. Eeek instead of white was a dirty musty grey color and looked drab and downcast. His nails were ragged and unkempt. Eek saw himself as a mess.

With courage in his heart Eek vowed to himself he would be clean or die in the attempt.

Eek walked to the creek and tried to bath. Eek did not know how to swim and stayed near the bank. Eek dared much and waded into the creek. Eek did have water cascade over him and started to feel clean. But since he had to stay in very shallow water he kept getting dirty and muddy each time he bathed.

Eek knew this was not the solution. Eek searched and found an outside small pool. Even the shallowest end was far too deep for Eek and he rightly feared that he pool would be his waterloo (Eek had eaten a tattered book about Napoleon) so Eek found a child's pail partly water-filled laying on its side but still had a small amount of water at the bottom since the pail was tilted on a piece of wood. Eek carefully tied a string tightly around his tail and tied the string end about a sturdy nearby blackberry bush, stopping and tasting and eating some berries to be full so he could float better; then Eek carefully slid into the pail and started to wash himself. A four year old girl came along and grabbed the pail. Eek thought he was a gone mouse but the girl tugged and pulled the string free and Eek, having his mouse ribs bruised, survived. He used his teeth to free the string from his now sore tail.

Over the next two weeks Eek had many adventures in his quest for cleanliness but to no avail.

CLEAN MOUSE

Eek found a large building and heard someone say in a singsong way "YMCA". The reminded Eek of a catchy song with the YMCA and he thought he would surely find a method to get clean in such a structure.

Eek then thought about the washer since he saw in the door that it had a frothy soapy atmosphere, but Eek rejected the washer since that also had a serious spinning motion and Eek was still too dizzy.

Slowly Eek putting one paw ahead of the other three searched the other rooms till he found the kitchen.

Eek did find much to drink and eat in the kitchen and for a short time thought to stop his quest for clean and stay in this kitchen. Eek admired the cleanliness of the kitchen and came back to the thought if this kitchen can be clean so can he.

With mouse resolve, Eek saw the dishwasher. It did not spin but was clean and soapy when running. Eek not only tolerated heat but actually enjoyed heat. Eek entered the YMCA dishwasher and within two cycles was cleaner than he had ever been.

Eek went to a mirrored surface and saw his new persona. He knew his former name had to go to the dust bin of history and soon named himself Squeaky, the clean mouse. The now named Squeaky the Clean Mouse had found his home and he remained the cleanest mouse in history, residing in a clean environment with ample food and drink and he could take a cleansing bath daily in the YMCA dishwasher.

TIPSY HIPPO

Brief background – Tom said the word "tipsy" but did not stop and added "hippo". I am not grateful to Tom due to this complication.

Tom was the circus trainer for large animals including a hippo. The second year the Hippo started to act tipsy or intoxicated and would actually fall down while performing. Some non-fan seeing probably a soul mate called out "Hey hippo you are tipsy!"

The name stuck and Hippo became known as the Tipsy Hippo. Tom delighted in this since he became the only trainer for Hippos and he thereby achieved his thirty moments of fame and had a lifetime job.

A learned Hippo expert determined that Tipsy Hippo was unstable and fell down from eating Russian potatoes which fermented in his stomach and made him drunk while Hippo. (In fact, several automobile drivers likewise where charged with DUI after eating potatoes, Russian or not.)

Unfortunately Tipsy Hippo soon had a tolerance for the Russian potatoes and refused to eat them spitting such out at passerbys and at Tom. Tom grew tired of spending money to have his uniforms cleaned and quit feeding Tipsy Hippo any potatoes. Tom used the Circus charge card to buy cheap Russian vodka and had Tipsy Hippo drink about a quart per day.

The circus found out and wanted Tom and wanted Tom to stop this expense Tipsy fell down one day and some probably tipsy person called out "HaHa -- Tipsy Hippo fell down and cannot get up".

Tom remembered the TV commercials where women were lying down and used the slogan "I fell down and cannot get up. Get medical alert today". Tom thought why not use a tipsy Hippo to do the same thing. (Authors interjection—Why did someone fall? Was it a stroke, heart attack or broken leg? Why could not that person get up? If someone helped how would that cure or fix the problem?)

TIPSY HIPPO

Tom actually knew a cousin of an uncle who was a partial friend of a little known politician who had ran for many offices but caught none who did a favor in childhood for the new third wife of someone who had a connection to the ad agency which handled this ad campaign for the non-profit which made the medical alert whistles or buttons or devices.

Leaving that on the floor, Tom was able to present the Tipsy Hippo commercial proposal. The not so mad ad men recalled there was a lizard selling insurance; Flipper selling who knows what; and many other animals, speaking or not, selling products.

Tom got the job for the test commercial to be the Hippo voice and practiced this in front of a triple mirror for a lengthy time period.

The commercial was shot in one take and Tom was great as the voice of Tipsy Hippo. However, this commercial never aired since Tom gave Tipsy Hippo too much vodka and Tipsy Hippo died.

TATTOO

Jeff and Josie were married and in a week they would be celebrating their third anniversary.

Jeff had before marriage a tattoo with a single purple rose on his left bicep. Of course, Josie had seen it and always recalled that Jeff told her that he had the tattoo created for the love he had with his high school girlfriend, Jennifer. During their first year of marriage, Josie asked Jeff to have his tattoo removed but Jeff was not willing to do so. Josie had a favorite flower, a lavender lilac and asked Jeff to get a second tattoo with a lavender lilac. Jeff would sort of say, "yes", but never follow through.

Josie did not have any tattoo and resisted Jeff when he asked her to get a tattoo depicting a four leaf clover.

Jeff decided to surprise Josie by having his rose tattoo removed and that would be his anniversary present.

Josie decided to surprise Jeff by getting a tattoo that Jeff wanted as her present for their third anniversary.

The evening before they told each other they had an errand to do and went to town and each visited separate tattoo parlors. Jeff did have his rose tattoo removed except for the stem and thorns. Josie did have a tattoo on her left thigh but somehow it was only a three leaf and not a four leaf clover.

Jeff wore a long sleeve shirt to hide the missing tattoo and Josie put on a pair of jeans rather than the skirt she usually wore. When they retired for the night, they took pains not to reveal their dual presents.

TATTOO

Jeff and Josie had decided to have a cozy at home catered supper and each promised to reveal their present at the end of the meal. Each gave the other a more mundane present, with Josie giving Jeff, an Xacto knife kit and a large model airplane kit since Jeff always recounted his pleasure when he was 10 years old building model airplanes. Jeff gave Josie two pairs of skates, roller skates and ice skates so she could engage in skating all times of the year. They were very happy and were looking ahead to starting a family the coming year.

When the meal was ended, both Josie and Jeff spoke at once and displayed their tattoo surprise. Both laughed at the absurdity of it, in effect, transferring tattoos but soon hugged and kissed with passion knowing that each of them wanting to please the other would take actions they had previously resisted.

They not only did have a happy marriage but made a point to take photographs depicting the tattoo of Josie and removal of the tattoo by Jeff. They eventually had four children and took delight in telling them about their wonderful third anniversary.

LIBRARY

Grace, who had never married and had no children, was 62 years old this rainy day in early September. Grace had been with the public library for 41 years having started when she was 21 and a new college graduate.

Reading was her life and hobby and urging others to read books was both her passion and mission.

It was a Saturday and the library was open from 10:00 a.m. to 6:00 p.m.

Grace had been the head librarian for some twenty years. A boy about ten years old came in dripping wet and Grace showed him the bathroom so he could get dry. Jared came out with his brown hair still wet and he timidly asked Grace: "Is there any book I can read while I am here until the rain stops? I saw this building all lit up and felt it was welcoming me. I cannot go home until after 5:00 p.m. so I thought I might read a book."

Grace asked Jared "What do you like to read?" Jared answered, "Mysteries –no picture or children's books or history or adventure books."

Jared also said this was the first time he had been at the public library and had no library card. Grace promptly took information from Jared and gave him a library card with his full name embossed.

Grace conversed with Jared in an adult manner and quickly learned that Jared could read at an acceptable level and provided him with a Perry Mason mystery by Erle Stanly Gardner, himself being a trial attorney, and a short history book giving a cursory history of the United States from the Revolutionary War through the Civil War.

Jared promptly sat in a comfortable library chair and said he would try to read both books before leaving the library. Jared also said that when he had two books he usually read some of each book and that was his method that rainy Saturday.

LIBRARY

Around one o'clock, Grace found Jared still reading and took him to the library cafeteria where Jared ate a good lunch. Jared gave Grace a one dollar bill and thirty five cents in change for the meal and Grace accepted this without comment.

Grace, after the meal, talked to Jared to see whether he was reading both books with comprehension and to her delight soon discovered that Jared did know each book very well.

Just after 4:30 p.m., Jared brought both books to Grace and said he was finished. Grace had already selected two other books and used Jared's library card to check them out. Jared was made aware that these books were loaned to him and must be returned on or before the stamped due date. Jared came to the public library most Saturdays and had interesting conversations with Grace. Grace always suggested to Jared what books or subjects to read and books to take on loan.

This scenario continued while Jared completed high school and by that time Grace had retired but she still volunteered at the public library. Grace made sure that she was there whenever she knew Jared would come by.

Jared went to college and upon graduating was drafted and served in the Army for two years. Jared then went to Law school. Jared and Grace used the old fashioned way since they actually wrote letters to each other while Jared was in college, serving in the Army and at Law School. Whenever Jared was home he made it a point to contact Grace and they often met at the library and had lively discussions.

Grace was in the County courtroom when Jared was sworn in as an attorney and she was present when Jared was elected City councilman at age 29. Grace was the featured guest when Jared married Susan and did see Jared at the hospital when each of his children, Joseph and Isabel were born.

LIBRARY

When Grace was 86 and Jared 34, Grace died at the public library from a massive stroke.

Grace in her will, left Jared her book collection. Jared spoke with elan at the funeral services for Grace and remarked "When I was a 10 yr. old black kid, I came out of the rain one Saturday and found the best friend I ever had—Grace the librarian".

PAPERBACK

Robert on a bright sunny day in May went to the public library for the two day surplus book sale. Robert was browsing when he spied a paperback book he had been seeking for some time. When Robert reached out to take possession of this paperback book, the hand without a ring thereon belonging to Karen who was visibly delighted to take this book.

Robert said to Karen , "You poached that book which I wanted", Karen said in a perky voice "Finders keepers and losers weepers."

Robert really wanted that book and took Karen b the elbow and they sat down to discuss this matter. Karen seeing how sincere Robert was offered a compromise "I will keep this book for one week and then you will have it for the next week."

Robert believed this a reasonable offer and accepted. They each paid fifty cents for the book and they sealed the bargain by writing in the flyleaf of the paper back their deal and signed it and set forth their telephone numbers.

The next evening Robert called Karen and they talked for about an hour without mentioning the paperback.

Robert did go on the internet but had no success in finding that paperback book. Karen did go to two local book stores but could not find a copy either. Robert and Karen did meet for lunch and dinner and started to date seriously. They did exchange the paperback book each week and thought it was almost a child and they had shared custody.

About two months later Robert suggested that they take it to a copy machine company and have a complete copy made. Karen agreed but then asked Robert "Who will have the original paperback?" Robert said "Why not play cards or dice or flip a coin?"

Karen said, "I have a better idea. Why not get married and jointly own and possess this paperback book since we both love it so much, we will never separate or get divorced."

PAPERBACK

Robert gave Karen a one word answer "sure". Robert and Karen did get married and merged their book and movie collections. They often said as their marriage flourished ((helped when they had three lively toddlers) "books have power and where would we be if we did not both love reading books and this paperback book brought us together and will bind us forever."

LOYAL

Ray met Julie when they were both six years old and attending Kindergarten. Tony, a smart-aleck seven year old pushed Julie into a sandbox and Ray came to her rescue. Ray was inept and Tony easily pushed Ray into the sandbox.

Ray and Julie took turns brushing sand off each other and shook hands. They pledged each other they would be forever friends and even though they did not know the word their loyalty to one another was cemented.

All through their school years they played together and supported each other. For any number of reasons, Ray and Julie never kissed; did give supportive hugs; helped each other and always were open and honest when conversing.

Ray became a carpenter and Julie achieved a MBA degree. They led separate career lives.

Each did attend the wedding of the other. They talked regularly on the telephone and did meet often for lunch. Dorothy, Ray's wife, and Brian, Julie's husband, not only accepted this friendly relationship but actively encouraged it.

After midnight, Julie was awakened by a frantic call from Ray. Julie told Brian that Ray needs to come to the house and talk to her. A few minutes later Ray did come in the kitchen and after having a large cup of plain coffee, told Julie the story: "I did tonight the most stupid thing I have ever done. Work has been slow and Dorothy has a broken arm so I, wanting to earn some money and listening to my friends, Charlie and Mike, drove my car while they robbed or rather tried to rob a 7-11 store. They have been caught and I do not believe they would turn me in. In fact, I do not know there is any belief by the police or the store employees that there was a third a person involved."

LOYAL

They talked for awhile and Julie said "Ray, I love you like a brother. You have to do the right thing and go to the police and confess. I will stand with you out of love and loyalty. Do this for your own sake. "

Ray knew she was right and went with Julie (accompanied by both Brian and Dorothy) and did confess.

Ray pleaded guilty and was given a one year sentence in jail with two years' probation and community service at the local public library. Dorothy did stand by Ray as did Julie.

Ray never did anything wrong in his life again. His marriage to Dorothy did prevail and they and their two children, Amy and Sue, did stay in that city and lived a good life. Ray made certain that Julie knew how much he admired and respected her for her enduring friendship and loyalty.

SOLACE

Shirley sought solace in solitude for six months following the death of her father, Jim. Shirley was walking down a street when she saw the well lit public library and felt the library was beckoning her.

Shirley had a library card and did go to the library on occasion.

A rather new employee, Victor, greeted her saying, "I am Victor. I am 26 years old and have recently quit my job as an automobile mechanic to live my dream and passion to work with books in this library. May I help you?"

Shirley replied, "I have been in solitude seeking solace for my grief but now I want to find solace in public and no longer in private."

Victor told Shirley "Why not come with me and we can together see what this public library has to offer." Shirley went with Victor and they looked at the shelves of new books but could find no "solace" books there.

Victor used the computer and entered the word "solace" and both were amazed to find some fourteen books with the title containing that word. Victor took a chance and suggested to Shirley that they should each take one of the "solace" books and sit together in the lounge area to read a few pages and have an amicable conversation. Victor had one hour lunch time and they went in to the lounge and sat reading for several minutes. Shirley found that Victor was easy to talk to and with and soon they were as old friends newly met.

Before parting, Victor asked Shirley to go out the next evening for a casual supper and Shirley surprised herself by agreeing.

Soon Shirley and Victor were dating. Both had never had a serious romance before and they found they had mutual likes and dislikes in music, art and books. They did have spirited and intense discussions. They found that by and large they did have shared values.

SOLACE

Not surprisingly, Shirley and Victor did fall in love. Nine months after their public library "solace" meeting they were married and had special permission to have their wedding ceremony in the library lounge.

Since their mutual love for each other and their deep enjoyment of reading books was ever present, they did have a happy marriage and welcomed with open hearts, the three children: Josephine, Harold, and Carl as each was born.

Shirley often thought to herself "solace indeed" while Victor thought "for sure-solace".

I AM HOMELESS AND.......

David, having turned 54 a few days ago, stood patiently in line waiting for the homeless shelter doors to open. It was a chilly day in September and David thought it would be good to get in the building, be assigned a cot for the night and in about an hour have a supper, his first real meal in two days. He knew he was lucky and perhaps wise to have arrived early. Since he had nothing to do, he had decided a warm bed and better yet a warm meal was worth his idle time.

While patiently waiting, David had snapshots in his mind of how he arrived at this desolate state of his life.

David had worked for some 24 years for the same company until the elderly widow of the owner was forced in effect to sell to a hedge fund and venture capitalist organization. Promises were made but not kept and within six months all the long term employees were fired. David did receive unemployment compensation for a year. Despite his resume and skills, David could not come close to finding a comparable job. Well before David exhausted his U.C. benefits, he found work at two part-time jobs. During that time the mortgage got paid. David tried to maintain his health insurance coverage but the full premiums required to be paid became too much for their limited budget and he found a bare bones health insurance with substantial co-pays and a yearly deductible of $10,000.00.

At that time, neither he nor his wife of 23 years, Julie, nor his son, Richard, age 16, nor his daughter Sally age 15, had any serious medical problems.

David still had his modest 401k plan funds which he wanted to keep for the future; to partially provide if possible for college education; and for retirement.

I AM HOMELESS AND ....

Just over a year previous disasters struck. First, his wife Julie cut her hand while cooking. Julie used the first aid kit and did go to the emergency room. She had eight stitches. This medical bill which was paid was over $1,500.00 since they had inadequate insurance coverage. During the next month, Julie had to return to the emergency department several times due to infection and other problems. Soon it got so bad that after a few more days Julie died. The total medical bills largely unpaid were in excess of $46,000.00. David cared for Julie for the time she lived and had during that time been terminated from one part-time job and gave up the second one.   In the meanwhile, the son Richard had a job with a fast food place and had to walk about a mile or so back and forth to that restaurant. Richard had a shortcut and two days after his mother died he was walking there in daylight when a random drive by shooting happened and he was struck by two bullets and died in the ambulance. The police told David at the funeral services for Julie that Richard was dead and had just been in the wrong place at the wrong time. Three weeks later, the daughter, Sally was a passenger and she died in an automobile collision when there was a driver swerving in front of a semi on the thruway causing the semi to veer and crash into several cars. Sally died from a crushed skull and other injuries.

David within one month lost through these tragedies his entire family. David was on only child and his parents had died some time ago. David had no close relatives. David turned to the father and sister of Julie for help but they were never close and lived several states away. David had due to many circumstances never been sociable and had no real friends.

I AM HOMELESS AND ....

David belonged to no church and always abhorred charity. David was overcome with depression and despair and over the next few months became more reclusive than ever. David did use his only savings the 401k plan to pay for the three funerals and to partially pay for the medical bills but ran out of funds. David did not apply for any governmental assistance.

The home was foreclosed on. The vehicle David had was stolen and he had no insurance. David had a yard sale and disposed of all furniture and personal property he and his family, now deceased, had.

The hospital seized his bank account, his last remaining financial asset. David had no means to keep up the limited health insurance policy so it lapsed.

David still waiting to enter the homeless shelter recalled what the last four months have been for him. He was homeless, unemployed, and seriously ill, with depression and disease. He survived by panhandling and using homeless shelters when available and soup kitchen meals.

David rarely bathed or kept up his appearance. He often thought he should act the way he felt; crazy ; and create such a public problem that he would be shot dead by the police as a perceived danger. David knew or thought he needed help but his

pride prevented him from seeking help. As he entered the shelter he thought, "I am homeless and ....

BLACK BOX

This is not intended to be a complete short story but it is similar to an outline to be presented to sell an idea for a movie or television show — but this is real.

Detailed outline:

1. Through some unknown scientific method anyone deceased can in fact actually be brought back to life for one hour.

2. The black box travels in multiples throughout the world and is 14 ft. wide by 24 feet long and ten feet high. It is divided into two sections and is very comfortable and well-designed. In one half the person(s) sit to talk to the dead. In the other section the deceased appears.

3. There is no physical touching. There is a barrier that is effectively air that prevents any physical interaction.

4. If desired the first ten minutes can be used for any verification of whatever he or she is called – is real.

5. For this situation the he or she will be called "One who answers true' or "Towat". Towat must answer truthfully and completely all inquiries. Towat can refuse to appear if Towat cannot for any reason answer truthfully.

6. The cost of this one hour discussion is two million dollars. One million goes to a local charity immediately before the one hour talk begins. All funds are paid in advance and held in an escrow account. The second million is for the business for all expenses and for profit. Worldwide there will be four units. About three days are needed to organize and complete each visit. When fully operations, there could be 8 visits per week times fifty weeks or a yearly total of 400/gross revenue will be eight hundred million

with half going to local charities. This can be expanded at any time by creating additional black boxes. .

7. If any interpreter is needed or expensive scientific tests need to be performed in that first ten minutes, these extra expenses at cost will be paid.

8. Anyone can use any audio or camera, etc. equipment but the there will not be any result due to the method to bring the Towat there is no known method to record in any media the one hour visit. Whoever pays for Towat visit can make a written verbatim record of what is said by using for example a court reporter. Regardless the actual words spoken by Towat cannot be reproduced.

9. Any Towat can be brought back for this one hour visit including anyone dead in the past who was a real person. There is no limitation except if the Towat will not come. Even then that Towat must state truthfully and completely the motive for not coming.

10. There will be free eight initial Towat visits by a lottery or other fair method. No money will be paid for the visit of Towat nor expenses. If a group wants to raise money for a legitimate local charity as part of these eight initial visits they may do so.

11. There is no method to prove that Towat, are real other than the test in the first ten minutes and the good faith and reliability of those who are selected to do these initial visits. There can be as many as six people in one half of the Black Box.

12. To reiterate, it is impossible to produce any audio or sound from Towat nor is it possible to record Towat by any method. Anyone can use any equipment to make such effort but this will prove to be impossible. The most sensitive devices can be used but will not pick up in any manner any trace of Towat. Person(s) who are in the

presence of Towat can hear and see Towat but cannot physically touch Towat. As stated during those first ten minutes any verbal test can be required of Towat or Towat will perform any conceivable physical test needed to prove that Towat is real. For example only, Madame Curie can be required to repeat any scientific experiment she did to discover radium. The same for Edison. The same for any artist for example a famous dead artist will paint on canvas a small portion of his or her painting. For example Hemingway can be asked and will answer anything asked to prove he is real for that one hour. Anyone can develop any test needed to prove that Towat is real.

THE IMMORTALS

There are immortals living in the world today. They are not superheroes; they have no super powers; they do not battle crime or tyranny. The immortals look like all others; dress the same; talk in the language of the country they are born in or live in; go to schools; marry and procreate children; work at meaningful jobs or not; are artistic or not; live in every aspect of life the same as everyone else except for one trait.

The immortals do not get any disease; not cancer; not heart disease; they are never sick in any way; they never go to a dentist since their teeth are perfect throughout their life. They never go to a doctor of health care facility. They need no medical exams nor blood test, etc. As part of any employment they still do whatever is required such as for that purpose only having a physical exam or blood test, etc. If they enter military service they have routine medical and dental exams.

When they are in the age range of 110 to 150, their external appearance is similar to a 30 or 40 year old. They age in appearance at about one fourth or less than the rate of others.

The immortals have no mental disorders or diseases. Some immortals smoke and drink alcohol. They very rarely commit any crimes but they are human. The immortals do marry and do divorce. The immortals are not financial wizards. Some are savers and some are spenders. The immortals are born in the usual manner but have no childhood diseases or medical or dental childhood problems.

The immortals belong to political parties; are biased or prejudiced; are in every manner and matter the same as all others except they are immortal so far as disease and illness are concerned .

The immortals do die of accidents, murder or suicide. The immortals do accept Medicare but never use it except for injuries so far as medical resources must be used.

Although rare, an immortal can beget an immortal child.

THE IMMORTALS

The only way to know that you have met one is that an immortal is never sick; never uses or needs medical or dental or mental health assistance (except for injury from accidents, etc.) Of course, an immortal since he or she can live to any age tends to grieve particularly upon the death of his or her spouse. The immortal plays sports, etc. but does so for a longer period of time. The immortal may very well work at employment much longer. An immortal can run for and be successful in politics. Immortals are sometimes creative and perform artistic endeavors such as being authors, painters, musicians, etc.

The immortal outlives all of his family members so far as spouse, children, and grandchildren, et al are concerned, except if such relative is also immortal.

No study has ever been done to determine the number of worldwide immortals. Since a rare few are born each year, the number of immortals does slightly increase. In some years the births exceed the deaths by accident, murder, and suicide and in some years deaths exceed births.

The immortals still live.

FOUR WAY PEDESTRIAN STOP

This peaceful small city, Solace, was a planned community that went much further than others. There was a planned downtown where the retail shops; services such as medical and dental; attorneys and CPA's; restaurants and cafés and theatres, etc. were all located. There were several small well maintained parks. By planning and city ordinances, in the outer ring absolutely essential vehicles are allowed for deliveries and needed services such as for physician visits.

There is an eight block by two and half blocks area where zero vehicles are allowed. There are no cars, trucks, bicycles, wheel chairs, strollers permitted. This area is for pedestrians only. The retail stores including grocery stores all deliver.

As part of the planning there are located certain areas just outside this area where pickups and deliveries occur.

Over the years the residents have grown to love this pedestrian only area and it has enjoyed some media attention. There are well-defined residential areas and sport venues and outer parks accommodate all who wish to sight-see and play. There are several tennis courts and three golf courses.

Hiram had been a council person for many years and had growing power on the five member council which governs this small city. The small police force has two family members who were nephews of Hiram.

During the past two years, Hiram had seen the popularity of the rectangle area grow and sometimes the crowd of people at the intersections was emulating the busiest corners of New York City. People were in a hurry and there was much jostling and pushing. Sometimes harsh words were spoken.

FOUR WAY PEDESTRIAN STOP

Hiram had a plan and unveiled it at the next council meeting. Hiram spoke; "I advocate the first in the nation four-way pedestrian stop. Here is the detailed ordinance. This will work just as a four way vehicle stop works. Pedestrians will gather at each corner. They will all wait for several seconds. Then clockwise the pedestrians on each corner will cross the street. This will be orderly and efficient. Any violation will be recorded both on video and cameras. The stop will be in operation seven days a week starting at 8:30 a.m. until 6:30 p.m. The first violation there shall be a $10.00 fine added to the residents tax bill. Increased fines will be imposed for subsequent violations. Repeat violators may have two added penalties—barred for a period of time from the rectangular area and/or a brief jail sentence."

Children under 12 years of age that violate this ordinance will have fines imposed on their parents and shall be barred from movies, sports, and entertainment for repeat violation for a time. Any visitors who violate this ordinance shall pay fines, etc. at once. We already have video/audio in this area and elsewhere with a manned central computer room at the local police building so there will be little additional expense to this city. Our efficient police force shall enforce with no exceptions this ordinance. The ordinance passed 4-1 after all legal matters occurred.

The local TV stations did a story on this first ever pedestrian stop and soon this went viral.

As time went on this stop became a tourist destination. A few rebels with or without a cause decided to test the ordinance by causing some havoc by jostling people and pushing and shoving. They were cited and when they repeated their antics and violations seven were placed in jail for three days and nights.

FOUR WAY PEDESTRIAN STOP

Due to this unique stop, congestion in the rectangle area substantially increased. Bus tours proliferated. Some people tested the resolve by attempting to ride skates, scooters and other devices to flaunt the ordinance. The evidence was clear based on the video/audio cameral records so that violators were caught and penalized.

A documentary movie was made of this unique area and was shown at select theaters throughout the nation.

It became quite a sight to see as many as fifty people lined up and crowding each of the four corners and similar to an old silent film starring Charlie Chaplin each group in sequence would walk, stroll, and proceed across the street. The wait time was sometimes a minute or longer. The city created several other four-way stops for pedestrians only in the rectangle downtown area. Informational signs were placed throughout the city regarding these pedestrian stops.

The city was proud of these stops and grew more prosperous. Other locations in the U. S. tried to copy this but had little success. This first four-way pedestrian stop was in history books and became enshrined in history.

POKER TELLS

The five men had played poker usually once a week for several years and each had tells -- observable distinct mannerisms that if observed could tell opposing players that the person was bluffing or had a good hand with regard to poker. Since all five had different tells the poker games were relatively equal so long as attention was focused.

Sam, a Pharmacist, was 43, married, and his poker game tell was the noticeable arching of his eyebrows when he had a good poker hand and sometimes but not always when bluffing.

Robert, 39, a lawyer, was recently divorced, and his poker tell was a continual pursing of his lips both when he had a good poker hand and when he was bluffing.

George was the oldest at 47, a CPA, and had in the last year remarried after his wife had died during their 22nd year of marriage and his poker tell was an act of repetitiously drumming his fingers. George had a different tempo when bluffing than he had when he had a good poker hand.

Phil was 44, an insurance broker, was married, but had a series of girlfriends that presumably his wife tolerated -- his poker tell was tapping as though to a tune with his feet and it became louder the more he bluffed or the better his poker hand. When such tapping was particularly loud and constant, the other four knew he had one of the best poker hands possible.

Richard, the youngest at 37, had never married, was the owner of two restaurants, and was thought to be gay. His poker tell was a habit he could not stop. When he had a good poker hand or was going to bluff, he used his left hand to repeatedly push a cowlick in his hair out of the way. When he tried to stop that tell it became funny since it was more pronounced.

POKER TELLS

The five played poker on a rotating basis at each others' home or apartment on Thursday evenings from 7 pm until 11 pm. By and large they were all prompt and rarely missed poker night. They quit sharp at 11 pm each time. The host furnished the beverages and the food. There was usually plain edible food. None of them were smokers so there was no smoking on poker nights. Four of the five were social drinkers but there were rarely any alcoholic drinks at poker night. In fact only Sam when he was the host offered drinks and usually there was little or no drinking.

The poker games for these five were serious and they all played to win. The host selected the poker game to be played. The ante was one dollar and the raises could never exceed five dollars each time.

The largest pot was over 500 dollars when all five stayed till the end and each of their poker tells were rampant since they all had what they considered very good poker hands.

George won with a full house, 3 Queens and 2 eights; Sam had three Kings; Robert had two airs; Richard had a lower full house, 3 nines and two sixes and lost; and Phil missed by one card having the best ever poker hand, an Ace high Royal Flush. Phil was the only one with a distinct poker tell who did not actually have a good hand and did the ultimate bluff which failed.

The five in addition to poker night often socialized. They had bowled together as a team for fourteen years in a bowling league. They were all excellent bowlers, not among the best and elite bowlers but very good second tier bowlers.

Each of them had one or more breakout years. Over the fourteen years they had bowled together, Sam had the overall average of 194; George has the highest game, a 288; Richard bowled the best series of 747; Robert had the best one year average of 204; and Phil constantly helped to win games by striking when needed. They won the league championship 6 times. They went to the ABC national championship held in different cities 11 times. They each did very well at several of their tournaments but they were never a threat to the tournament champs.

POKER TELLS

There were arguments between them particularly when Sam, a lifelong Democrat, and Phil, a recent convert of the Republican Party debated politics. They had ruled out any real discussions of religion and placed a limit of 10 minutes on political discussions. There were no serious rifts or animosity or jealousy between them. They were by all accounts good friends and when one had a serious problem, the others helped with advice, and comfort and if ever needed, money.

The poker nights were sacred to them and although they played to win it was a true pleasure for them to be together and poker night above all else was fun.

DIVISIVE COUPLE

Alex had for thirty five years before retiring with a full pension at age 62, and having paid for health care for himself and his wife, Regina, age 58, until they qualified for Medicare, had spent his working days on a consistent pattern. Alex rarely missed a day re: his teaching position where over the years he taught history at the local public school in grades 10 through 12. He enjoyed teaching. In addition for the past 24 years he was the assistant music teacher not only at his school but also when called upon part time at four other schools.

Most work days he did not come home till close to 6 pm. He was usually fatigued and he and Regina rarely went out on weekdays except to visit their adult children or grandchildren.

They had by the time Alex retired four children, three who lived in their area. Often on the weekends they would go visiting their children and often would take care of one or more of their five grandchildren.

Alex had two passions, to travel and to listen to Opera. Many evenings, Alex would play an opera from his collection. Sometimes he would read one of his books on Opera.

A few times a year an Opera performance would come to his city or in an area where he could go up to a 50 mile radius. Most times Regna would accompany him and seemed to enjoy the opera and music.

Before retirement they rarely did much traveling. Alex in the several years prior to his retiring told Regina what a great life they would have traveling to opera venues and going to Europe and Russia and China and to South America.

The major thing that Alex planned was to buy a large travel trailer and travel throughout the United States to meet up at campgrounds with other opera lovers. Also to tour the U.S. and visit wherever live opera shows were being performed.

DIVISIVE COUPLE

Regina never said anything to Alex until about six months before his scheduled retirement when he had made an appointment at the highly rated travel trailer dealership to buy a travel vehicle. At that time Regina said she would not help Alex to select one and for the first time told Alex she had no intention of traveling far away and for lengthy times. Regina said she was quite happy to stay home and visit with the children and grandchildren.

Alex asked Regina if she tolerated the Opera or did actually enjoy opera. Regina finally said she cared little for Opera but went along with Alex since he enjoyed opera so much. Regina also told Alex none of the children liked opera.

Alex thought differently but came to realize that he had to choose -- his family in accord with Regina and only play opera at home and see operas rarely or fulfill his passion for both Opera and travel.

Over the next twelve years Alex traveled alone in his travel trailer all over the United States, twice on extended trips to South America, four times for months to Europe, China and Russia.

For over ten months each year Alex was on the road. Often he would preplan campground visits where he would meet up with other traveling opera lovers for several days and nights.

Alex believed he had married Regina for better or worse and had no intention of legally separating or divorcing her.

Alex always was home for a period of time each year at Christmas and when there were planned special occasions. Alex provided very well financially for Regina. He used investments and savings to pay for his travel and expenses and to that extent cut into the "inheritance" for his heirs.

Most times Alex was in the company of couples who did travel together and had a passion for opera. Sometimes he met men often older than himself whose story was similar -- if married the wives either did not like opera much or loathed traveling.

DIVISIVE COUPLE

Sometimes there would be a single female traveling who loved opera but usually women would travel in a pair or threesome. Alex often thought of himself as having a low sex drive since on all of his travels he was never tempted to stray or in any way to violate his marital vows.

Alex wrote three well received books detailing his extensive travels and intertwining his profound love of opera.

When Alex was 71, he suffered a severe stroke thus ending his traveling. To the end of his life however, which was for ten more years, he spent much time enjoying his opera collection and remembering his wonderful travels.

MOTIONLESS CATTLE

In this part of the country, Highland Cattle were a novelty and a curiosity. These large shaggy cattle were unique since not only did the bulls have large curved horns sharpened to a point for goring things when needed, but so did the heifers and calves. The calf's initially had knobs on their heads which became horns.

For some time, people would stop and inquire about the Highland Cattle. The cattle by and large were docile and other than crushing one against a fence or possibly using their horns they were tame.

Schools regularly made field trips to see these cattle and many of the new born calves became in effect pets.

The farm became an outdoors zoo to some extent.

One day a gifted amateur photographer requested permission to create a photographic record of the Highland Cattle. Permission was granted and help from the owners was freely offered to restrain the cattle and to assist in positioning them to the extent needed.

The cattle were not used to being prodded to "pose" and wanted to move around freely.

Many photos were taken of the cattle in various stages of motion.

The female photographer, Lynn, asked if she could take a panoramic photo of the cattle by having some kneel down, others standing up and the young ones in the front. What was sought was a family cattle portrait.

The owners agreed and with much effort, such a Highland Cattle family portrait was accomplished. Several exposures were done while the cattle for the time were motionless. Lynn commented that if only she could take family photographs of humans who usually twitched, moved around and rarely were motionless as these cattle were, she would be very happy.

MOTIONLESS CATTLE

Lynn promised and delivered a booklet of the photographs. The owners decided that some were so good including the motionless family Highland Cattle photo, that they would have several enlarged to cattle size and use the family one as a billboard at the entrance of the farm.

They, Tim and Ruth, and their teen children, Amy and Brad, made it a point to show the cattle the family cattle sized photos.

One young bull, Sylvester, stared at himself in the photo and became motionless for a time. Soon the other cattle did likewise. The next time a busload of 4th graders visited the farm on a field trip, the cattle did their act and stood motionless. In seemingly no time, the motionless cattle who posed for people and photos became a media sensation.

The farm, never prosperous, became very efficient and wealthy since admission was charged and non-believers came from all parts of the world to view and study cattle who had the intelligence and ability to become motionless when they wanted to and without any training.

SCHOOL EXPERIMENT WORDS

Lorraine, the second grade teacher, told her class of 22 students one sunny day in October: "We are doing something different today." Please do the following:

1. Do not put on the sheet of paper your name or anything that would identify you. This whole matter is to be anonymous -- a mystery that no one will know.

2. Write down five different words. Think about what the five words mean to you.

3. Then consider which word sounds best to you or is your favorite or is most important and circle that one word.

4. Marcie, you are to gather up the papers and put them on my desk.

5. I will then take these 3 x 5 cards and print out each word on a separate card.

6. Richard will then come up and shuffle the cards and hand each of you a card keeping the last card for himself.

7. If anyone receives a card with a word that he or she wrote, I want those students to raise their hand.

8. Take the card home and this evening your after school assignment is to write a fiction, story that is, not a true story using that word.

9. This is not a test but is an experiment. During the next several days each of you will read to the class your story placing emphasis on the word on each of your cards.

The students all complied and after Richard had doled out the cards, Lorraine said, "I will tell you how I came up with this idea. I saw a man with a billboard slung over his shoulders with a sign that said, "Tell me a word and I will tell you a story.""

Lorraine then related to the class that very few approached the man but as she watched a few did.

Lorraine did talk to this man and asked him why he was doing this. The man responded that he loved to tell stories and he thought this would be a unique way to do so.

SCHOOL EXPERIMENT WORDS

The man asked Lorraine what word she chose and she said, "Jewel." For a few minutes the man spun out a story about a jewel which was exciting and unique and unexpected.

This tale stuck with Lorraine all summer and so she decided to use it for this class.

Lorraine while writing each word on the cards thought this would enhance some of the students in their use of words and also enable some of them to write a story. She had told the class that they should use their abilities and imagination and write a story that appeals to them. Lorraine said: "Be not afraid. Write any story that you can think of. There is no right story or wrong story."

Authors Note: I could tell readers what 22 words were on the cards and if there were any duplicates but you, that is, anyone reading this -- make up your own list of 22 words and then create a story from the one word which most enthralls you. Do it and see what happens.

SHEEP WHO QUIT "BAAING"

The twelve contented sheep, ewes, Sally; Sheryl; Samantha; Sybil; Sherry; Arabella; Beatrice; Caroline; Dorothea; Eliza; Felicia; and Gertrude, were all over two years old and had lived on the farm owned by Theodore and Teresa since they were acquired through a 4H auction. Their language was "BAA" -- with several degrees of loudness and tones.

However, Theodore and Teresa, on hearing any and all "baas" interpreted those as requests to be fed and ignored those "baas" which were intended to communicate other matters such as illness -- danger from predators -- weather changes -- that one or more of the sheep were trying to escape and might be injured and killed. One "Baa" that each sheep bleated meant they were happy and had sincere sheep love for both Teresa and Theodore.

As stated Theodore and Teresa only recognized "baas" as food requests so they lost out on all the other "baas."

Eliza woke up one morning and made a different sound -- it was close to a bark that the dog, Stella, emitted. Eliza was excited and barked at the other sheep. Getting their attention, Eliza stood in the circle of sheep and told them reverting to the "baa" language about her bark. Eliza told the other sheep that they should learn other ways to express themselves -- such as different barks as dogs do; many of the different meows similar to cats; neighing as horses do; chirping in many ways that birds do; the voice sounds of woodpeckers; the sounds that roosters and chickens make; the roars and sounds of the Highland cattle.

The sheep thought this was a great idea and the all quit saying "baa" and each started to use other animal language and sounds.

Theodore and Teresa came to feed the sheep and did not hear any "baas" but instead the sheep used barks, meows, neighs, chirping etc. instead. Teresa and Theodore were amazed and enthralled by the novel sounds emitting from the sheep.

SHEEP WHO QUIT "BAAING"

They brought recording equipment in and recorded a day in the life of the sheep. They contacted a nearby University which provided degrees in animal husbandry and played the recordings for the faculty. All of the faculty were skeptical and did not believe.

The faculty and selected students were invited to the farm. They came -- they observed the sheep -- they listened and heard the sheep communicating -- they studied and researched -- they left convinced that these sheep had quit "baaing" and had somehow learned to use other animal voices and sounds to communicate.

Eventually a video with sound was made and it went viral. A well received documentary was made.

The farm became very prosperous from admission fees and tourist visits. No one ever determined how the sheep quit "baaing." Only Eliza knew but never told.

TRUE NEIGHBORS

One evening Elaine was sitting with her husband, Frank by the fireplace. It was February and it was cold and snowing. As often happened since their children were adults and had their own lives to live, they talked about old memories.

Elaine raised the subject of <u>true neighbors</u>. Frank said, "Remember when I was laid up and George came over wanting to mow the lawn with our new John Deere lawn tractor." Only I had ridden it and I knew Frank, being the klutz he is would wreck that tractor. You remember that I told him we were experimenting to see how high the grass would grow. George bought that story and he bugged me several times as to how high the grass grew. I had to, with some effort, go out, and measure the lawn and I then despite my aches mowed the lawn.

To top it off, when I told George how high the grass grew, he said he went around to the neighborhood and measured their grass. To shut him up I told him our grass was imported and we had the record for the height of our grass.

Elaine then culled her memory and related how Annie, our now deceased neighbor, had heard that Elaine was ill with the flu and in bed. Annie brought over for six days in a row that awful split-pea soup with the secret ingredients that her great- great- great- great aunt supposedly had fed Indians and they liked that soup so much that it was featured in their dances and rituals. Our ancestors go back a long way in this area and I do not know of any Indians here. But her heart was good and I listened to her tale of the soup.

"Frank," said Elaine, "you remember how sick I was when I actually ate part of that smelly, rotten tasting split-pea soup."

Annie believed in that soup and she brought it over for the next five days. I did my trick of having a coughing fit so I did not have to eat that vile concoction. "You remember I fed some to our cat, Matilda, and she became very ill. Annie was a good neighbor and person and despite that soup was a <u>true neighbor</u>.

Frank asked Elaine why do you refer to neighbors we have had over our more than forty-five years as "true."

TRUE NEIGHBORS

Elaine responded that they have been fortunate to never having what would be considered bad neighbors. However many were what could be called silent neighbors since rarely would you even know they existed. Those silent ones never caused trouble, were polite but did not go out of their way to be friendly.

True neighbors are those who are there for you, inquire with feeling how you are; are interested in you; and whatever crisis happens are the first ones to respond with needed help. You can tell a <u>true neighbor</u> a secret and they will not gossip. With a <u>true neighbor</u> you can reveal your feelings and they will provide a shoulder to cry on and arms to hug you. We have had many true neighbors.

Frank told Elaine, "Let's go to bed." Remember all the times you have been a <u>true neighbor</u> to others. Since you are a <u>true neighbor</u>, I believe others in return are <u>true neighbors</u>.

LOVE

Isaac woke up one morning, as usual; first thinking that it was better to wake up than not to; and then for an unknown reason, his next thought was, "love."

Isaac had been married to Maria for some 46 years when she died of fast growing cancer about three years ago.

Isaac never had any desire to find another woman to love.

Running through his head was that love was the best four letter word. There are many good and bad four letter words and word itself is one of them.

While making his normal breakfast of a glass of water; cereal with fruit; and toasted rye bread, Isaac thought more seriously of the word "love."

He knew no one who could with absolute certainty define "love." We all believe we see love when eyes flash and bodies want to merge and we say "they are in love" but of course they may actually be in lust.

Many people marry and fall into real love gradually. Humans do profess love for animals and some do love animals more than they love babies.

Isaac knew with every fiber of his being that although like many he loved Maria with his heart logically he loved Maria with his brain since the heart has no emotions.

He thought about how profound the word "love" is since it is extolled in movies, television, books and thoughts probably more often and with more emotion than any other word.

Isaac then went back to his memories. When he was very young although the emotion of love he remembered having he did not spend any time thinking about it. He tried to be totally honest in remembering his early days and nights with Maria and whether in fact it was love at first sight which he often said it was. He knew that one of the happiest days in his life ever was when he nervously proposed marriage to Maria. He believed he was the "one" for her and she was the "one and only" for him. He could not begin to imagine what his life would have been if Maria said "no."

LOVE

The answer was a robust yes and in his view Isaac and Maria did love one another and their marriage was not a fairy tale but was truly happy.

About six years ago, Isaac was very ill and he was dying. Maria held his hand and constantly hugged him. She implored him t live and he has always believed that her love made him live.

Isaac then with sorrow in his heart (brain actually) remembered in vivid detail the awful eight weeks that Maria suffered till she mercifully died. After Maria told Isaac to go on with his life after she died, she, with her last breath told Isaac that she knew he was the "one" for her and she loved him the instant she saw him.

Isaac feeling a little tired having spent time thinking of the word "love" and retaining as always the memories of Maria went on with his life.

SOCIETY FOR DEBATE RE: UNESSENTIAL MATTERS

The society met as scheduled. Sam, the temporary "chairperson" for three months so far, asked all to come to order. Actually their existence in this Society was always out of order and intended to be such.

Sam said, "As we voted at our last session we are to announce here and now our one word which we believe is the best word in the history of people. As I call out your names you will be silent or announce your word choice. When we have listed all of them you will then be requested to vote for your first and only choice. The five words selected then will be set up for debate at our next meeting with members chosen to affirmatively espouse by debate their word. At the conclusion of that debate, all present will again vote and the best word in history will be historical. What you do with this information and ultimate selection is your unessential decision.

George -- Loyalty	Ralph -Conservatism	Ruth -- Happiness	
Tom -- Love	Linda -- Friendship	Louis -- Democracy	
Louise -- Children	Cathy -- Like	Dorothy -- Voting	
Tony -- Charity	Zack -- Hope	Charles -- Need	
Mary -- Mercy	Brenda -- God	Cheryl -- Religion	
Bill -- Beauty	Donald -- Faithful	Regina -- Vows	
Harold -- Dictomy	Marilyn -- Sex	Judy -- Space	
Jerry -- Unknown	Carol -- Mystery	Dan -- Question	Ray -- Art

After a very spirited discussion the society voted by a majority that the words to be debated would be:

God -- Love -- Democracy -- Hope -- Question

A cadre of three volunteered to debate each of these words.

Sam uttered the last sentences since this was one of the few perks of his temporary position.

SOCIETY FOR DEBATE RE: UNESSENTIAL MATTERS

"We as a society will advertise this profound debate and use the donated venue to have the public attend and see for themselves that unessential matters can be deep and meaningful."

"Make certain that you, the debate teams hone your verbal skills and write as much as you need to have cogent well reasoned arguments." "Go forth to win this Debate."

(To be Continued)

DEBATE

The evening arrived for the debate sponsored by the Society for Debate Re: unessential Matters and Sam was happy. In addition to the 37 members of the society, almost 100 spectators were there.

Sam retold the simple rules:

1. Each team of three members had to prepare a debate written document no longer than five typed double spaced single pages espousing their word as the best word in history. Each team could divide up the time they spoke in favor of such word any way they desired. Each team had five minutes to speak initially and two minutes in rebuttal. Time will be strictly adhered to with a warning bell one minute before the end of the five minutes and 15 seconds before the two minute rebuttal.

2. The teams will be chosen at random both with regard to the initial and rebuttal debates.

3. The general public each has a form with the words printed on and can at the conclusion of the debate vote within five minutes in what order they cast their vote. These will be tallied promptly and the public vote announced.

4. The 37 members of the society will also provide a written vote ranking the words in order of choice.

5. The words as set forth on the overhead visual screen are:

Democracy   God   Hope   Love   Question

The debate commenced and part of the debate including the rebuttal were:

Hope -- Everyone needs hope in their personal lives. Hope makes life worth living. If a person loses hope he or she will surely die in medical situations. If a person loses a relationship and then ceases to have hope, that person is doomed to have a very unhappy life. Hope is good and needed.

DEBATE

Democracy -- Of course there are different phases of democracy but the fundamental principles are the same: Democracy requires freedom to peacefully protest -- to speak -- to live without fear of arrest etc. if one's thoughts or beliefs are at odds with that of the prevailing government -- to freely worship -- to be able to vote. Without democracy, people can never be happy and thrive.

Question -- Science, medicine, law, the human fabric would be at an end if persons could not question. The essence of asking questions and desiring to find answers has driven people to explore the land, the sea, and space. All human progress in every field of endeavor requires and demands questions and the endless seeking of answers. Ask yourself what would now be if people did not question. It is essential to life.

God -- The concept of God is entwined with Religion, both freedom of religion and the search for the meaning of life. Faith and belief in power of prayer is needed to have the idea of God. It is admitted that religion and fervor regarding this has caused and will cause endless strife, wars and deaths. But the failures of religion only establish the doctrines of free will and how profound religion is in many lives but it does not in any way refute God as a word, an idea, or a belief.

Love -- Without love, life for most would be barren and devoid of meaning. How can one have Hope without Love? How can one question devoid of love on or in the brain. How can one even conceive of God unless Love is part of and the essence of God? In what way can democracy flourish if people do not Love. It is said that Love makes the world go around but it would be better to state that one who is without love does not exist. Love clearly is the best word.

The public attendee votes were tallied as well as the votes of the 37 members of the society.

DEBATE

The words in their order both by the society and the public were the same but with different percentages:

Debate Voting Chart

Word	Public	Society
Hope	17%	15%
Democracy	21%	20%
Question	18%	21%
God	21%	20%
Love	23%	24%

Therefore by a slim margin Love was voted the best word in History.

CAMPS

Five men, ranging in age from 61 to 64, Tom, Richard, Harold, Bruce and Chuck had several things in common. Except for Richard who had inherited money when his parents died in an airplane crash when he was 20, all others earned their wealth. Each had served either in the Military or the CIA for many years. Each had killed multiple times the enemies of the United States. Each could be deemed Macho but caring at least regarding their wives and children. None were particularly mean or cruel but each stood their ground re: both their personal lives and their business interests.

They came from diverse backgrounds and maintained strong positions on political and social issues. They never discussed their religion and they did have respect for the diverse political stance each had.

They essentially had similar moral values.

Over time they and their families became good friends and they had invested heavily in different business ventures.

Richard and Tom were heavy smokers and except for Bruce on occasion they drank too much. They protected each other and if anyone was threatened in any manner the others had their back.

This however is not the story of their lives and adventures which might be written in the future but it is concerning the time they jointly visited a 2,000 acre land parcel that Tom and Bruce thought could be developed.

In their weekend discussions they came to the decision to create a corporation to buy and own this acreage. By pooling their considerable resources they could easily buy this land with cash and they did.

At first they thought of one camp for hunting and fishing. But Harold and Chuck came to the meeting and proposed developing this land into five camps.

CAMPS

Their vision was that there would be a large parking area with one large welcome building so that each of the theme camps would be serviced by multiple roads which would then be constructed taking each group of campers to their destination camp.

The camps were as follows:

1. Hunting -- Bruce.

2. Fishing -- Harold.

3. Newlyweds (romantic) -- Chuck.

4. Survival -- Tom.

5. Mystery Camp -- Richard.

They all participated in the design and layout and building of the five camps. They often called this concept, "Other World Camps."

The name chosen for the site was, "Camps without Limit." The five separate camps were named in accord with their primary use and goal.

Each camp would be on about 300 acres. The hunting, fishing, and survival camps were rustic. Each had a state of the art virtual reality area where hunters and those who fished and wanted survival skills could go and realize their dreams. For example, the fishing virtual area allowed fishing aficionados to be in the rapids catching salmon or having the thrill of deep sea fishing for sharks or Tarpon. Hunters could go on terrifying safari hunts for lions or tigers.

The newlywed camp would spare no expense in being the ultimate venue for romance.

All the camps would have world class cuisine and service. At any one time the limit would be strictly enforced as to the number of campers so there would be zero crowding. Security would be first class. One night at any of the camps would be $1,500.00 per person.

CAMPS

With regard to the Survival camp this would also include urban survival teaching such as car chases - weapons etc. There would be the basic survival camp at one price and a much higher price paid regarding evasion tactics and urban survival skills.

The mystery camp would be unique. Every visitor -- guest -- would receive intensive orientation and then blindfolded and taken on a scary ride to their secret destination.

Twice a year the mystery theme would be changed and with considerable expense would be well planned to give the guests what they really want -- a unique mystery experience sometimes scary -- sometimes filled with laughs.

It took eighteen months to build these five camps so they would open at the same time. Major efforts were made to recruit personnel. A guest at any of the camps had to be an adult. Of course only married newlywed couples could come to the newlywed camp. However, same sex married newlyweds were also welcomed. As was true of their other business ventures, the "Camps without Limit" was very successful.

THE APPROACH

Larry 20 years old, had not had a date for two months and was despondent. Larry had graduated from High School and never had any desire to attend college. He was still living at home with his parents, Sue and Henry, his younger brother, Andrew, 18 and three sisters, Sarah, 19, Suzette, 17, and Sally the youngest, age 16.

Larry was the manager of the 24 bowling lanes business and he bowled for several years in two leagues. He had worked at the bowling lanes for over five years and had been assistant manager in his senior year and a year ago had been promoted to manager. His paycheck went up by 50%.

His duties were to manage the finances and business at the bowling lanes and the pro shop and the connected restaurant.

The corporation which owed these business had many additional business interests and Larry was told, "Succeed here and in a year or so you will have a promotion and earn double or more your present salary."

Larry was a good businessman and had self-confidence.

Larry was almost six feet tall, slim of build, had wavy brown hair and brown eyes. His face was not memorable but when animated he did have a friendly smile.

Larry had obtained a book of short stories and one evening was struck with a story of a fellow who traveled the world and approached total strangers, saying, "Give me a word and I will tell you a story." Despite being rebuffed often the man, named Sam, sometimes was told a word and in two minutes related a story using that word.

Larry liked that story and spoke out loud to himself, "Tomorrow night I am going to use this approach as my method to find a woman to date." "I can tell a story most likely and if given time actually write a story."

THE APPROACH

The next evening Larry introduced himself to a group of young women who had finished their league bowling and were having a meal. Larry told them he was the manager and then asked the redhead, Gladys, to tell him a word. Gladys amused thought and then said "cloud." Larry said he would write a short story and give it to Gladys and if she then agreed, he would ask her for a date.

Gladys then said, "I am not attracted to you now but this approach is different." "If I get good vibes from the story I will accept a date with you."

Larry left and the five women, Gladys, Brenda, Yvonne, Teresa, and Wallis had Larry's approach as a conversation subject.

During the following week, Larry started and threw away seven stories. He finally decided to make it simple and he wrote a story about how clouds and their shapes might inspire a young girl to take up painting.

The next evening Larry went to the table where Gladys and the others were waiting for their after bowling meal. Gladys told Larry, "I will read this in private and come back with my decision." A few minutes later, Gladys came back and told Larry that this approach was novel but she did not feel any real attraction to him and rejected his overture. She added that perhaps if he tried this approach in a one and one situation that it might be successful.

About an hour later when Larry was having his coffee, he looked up and said, "You are Yvonne, right?" Yvonne sat down and told Larry, "I will tell you a word now and you can tell me a story." "I am interested in you and your novel approach." "The word is "absolute."" Larry paused and then said, "Absolute is a word like eternal, implying certainty." "I am enthralled by you uttering that word but am a little intimidated also since I think I will have to work very hard to keep up with you." "I will have to now study the word "absolute.""

THE APPROACH

Larry and Yvonne spent the next enjoyable hour conversing about their lives. Yvonne, 21, was a paralegal in a law firm, was also still living at home, was 5 ft. six inches tall, had an athletic build, and had blue eyes and blondish hair. When interested as she was with Larry, she smiled often and had a truly welcoming smile.

Before leaving, Larry asked and Yvonne accepted that they would go to a movie and dinner Saturday evening.

OLDEST AGENT

A few days after Fred had his 91st birthday and more than a year after the death of his wife of 64 years, Doris, he entered CIA headquarters. Fred met with two CIA supervisors who enroll new CIA agents.

They, Roger, and John, showed Fred his file. They knew all the facts of his life. Fred told them he wanted to serve his country; he did not fear death; he was willing to kill when needed.

Roger told Fred that he could be a solo agent and since he was signed up for a tour of Europe to start two weeks later and which would last for 21 days, Fred would be in an excellent position to perform one or more missions. The tour manager was in the employ of the CIA and would cover for Fred when he had to be absent from the guided tour.

John added, "Fred - you are the oldest agent ever." "We need you and will depend on you."

Fred received detailed instructions and was outfitted with spy equipment.

The tour manager, named Sam, and the group numbered 15, two married couples, and 11 singles, both men and women met the night before their flight to Paris where the seven country tour would begin.

Fred was not to spy on the tour members since they had been fully vetted. They were all over 65 with Fred being the oldest. They were all healthy and able to walk well.

Fred did know three of the singles, Amy, Alice, and George. For almost three hours Fred mingled with all of the tour members and spent time with Sam so they could make necessary arrangements so that Fred could carry out his missions for the CIA. The tour was to include Paris; Berlin; Oslo; Copenhagen; Barcelona; Vienna and Venice with about three days at each city.

At each city there were planned guided tours of famous places, and entertainment with scheduled dances and parties.

Fred could have sufficient time to carry out his missions and he would have to have at most a few hours three times when he would plead fatigue or a bad cough as an excuse.

Everything proceeded like clockwork and the three absences of Fred were little noted.

When Fred arrived home, he spent several hours being debriefed. During this 21 day tour, a terrorist plot was thwarted in Berlin with the arrest of several in Berlin and London. The second terrorist plot ended with no damage and this one started in Venice and involved many cities in Europe.

These involved extensive investigations but Fred, although present at each event, was not recognized nor detained.

Fred also told Roger and John that six foreign agents which were his targets died. Two fell off buildings; one drowned; one was killed in a hit and run auto accident; one was knifed in an apparent mugging with the last one shot and killed.

All of these deaths did receive some publicity and some were being actively investigated. There was no hint or mention of Fred relating to the plots or deaths.

What Fred revealed to Roger and John was and still is classified. They gave Fred a computer thumb drive and told Fred that he could undertake another mission if he wanted to. Fred said he could consider this.

When Fred went home he was interviewed by Sally, the reporter for the local newspaper. The paper had reported his attempt to be the oldest CIA agent previously.

Fred, as all agents do, lied primarily by omission asserting he was rejected. But he did tell Sally many tales about his 21 day tour and provided her with several photographs.

Fred also briefly mentioned how exciting it was to be where two terrorist plots were discovered and he ignored any mention of the six deaths that occurred by coincidence in cities that the tour was at.

OLDEST AGENT

Fred fondled the thumb drive in his pocket and thought, "maybe and why not."

BAT REBELLION

Batty had been a bat all his life and as other bats did he only flew around at night. He wondered why he could not fly during the day. It would be warmer and to fly and soar in sunlight and to see the sun and clouds, Batty thought would be exciting.

Batty started to detest flying at night when it was so dark and scary. Also, he had to evade owls and other night predators.

Using his squeaky bat voice Batty talked to other bats and soon had a substantial number advocating flying in the daylight.

That Sunday, just as the sun went down, the bats convened a bat meeting. They all hung around upside down as usual until Batty and several other bats said in their squeaky bat voices, "We are going to perch upright and quit hanging upside down with our heads down." "We demand to stand tall." "Furthermore, when the sun comes out tomorrow, we are all flying in daylight and we are going to sleep at night."

This caused an uproar and most of the senior bats squeaked in opposition. There were warnings that if Batty and the others flew with the sun the old proverb would be true, "Blind as a Bat." They also warned about all of the dangers of daylight such as cats and dogs and other animals. Also, how would Batty and the others feed themselves?

After an hour or so, Batty spoke up, "Have any of you bats ever tried to fly in the daylight?" "All you are warning is bat lore and it is not even in writing." "We are going no matter what danger there may be." "We are now going to get a good night sleep so we can be alert at sunrise."

Batty and his comrades retired for the night and had to fall asleep hanging upside down. Batty had a last thought that in addition to flying in the daylight he would learn to sleep on his back or side and not upside down.

The next morning Batty and his group prepared to fly. The remaining bats were hanging around asleep since they had flown at night.

BAT REBELLION

Batty et al flew towards the sun and did acrobatic maneuvers. Initially, they had difficulty adjusting their eyes so they flew slowly and carefully. At first children and then adults saw the strange to them sight of bats flying in the day time. Batty stayed away from rural areas where farmers might shoot them down. Batty and other bats found food similar to what they normally ate. Batty found a park where people were feeding pigeons and birds and landed and were fed.

Some people had never seen a bat.

Batty flew in an open window and woke up a girl, five years old, and squeaked to her and landed on her arm. The girl and Batty spent a few minutes together and Batty flew out the window.

Batty had told the other bats they would only fly around through lunchtime and they did, and they enjoyed a feast of leftovers. Actually the bats ate so much at lunch they were loggy and had some trouble flying. As planned, they returned to their bat abode and spent the rest of the day relating their positive memories of their daylight flight adventures.

Batty, before going to sleep, thought: "I have now flown in the daylight and am going to learn to sleep on my back." "Maybe, just maybe, I can learn to write so that all bats can discover the sheer joy of flying in daylight." "Also, I am going to visit that girl again and I heard her name is Pandora and maybe she will open her box she had on top of her dresser."

TYPEWRITER MAN

Jerry on his eighth birthday received what he considered his best ever present. This was an electric Royal typewriter. It was May and Jerry was bored at school. He practiced day in and day out to learn to use two fingers to type and he did become somewhat adept at typing.

Before summer started he typed seven short stories and for an unknown reason to him Jerry could not even start an eighth story. Jerry put his typewriter away and during the years till he graduated from high school, Jerry would use a different typewriter and would write/type seven more stories or writings but he could not type the eighth one and had to obtain another typewriter to continue.

In college, he had a Smith Corona electric typewriter but the same thing happened but became worse since he, after typing seven writings such as required essays, could not type anymore on that typewriter, no matter how hard he tried. He took that Smith Corona and stored it in the attic with the Royal one.

Jerry got by in college by using friends' typewriters and using the college typewriters or computers. Each time he could not type more than seven writings on any one typewriter, or computer.

Jerry graduated with a BA and an MBA and became a successful businessman. He did marry and had three children.

By the time Jerry was 35, he had bought thirty seven typewriters which he had lined up on tables. Jerry had a hobby of writing short stories and they were stored in a filing cabinet. No matter what Jerry did he could only type seven writings or stories on any one typewriter. Other family members had no difficulty with using and typing on any of the 37 typewriters.

Jerry had the typewriters checked by several experts but they were all baffled and had no explanation.

Jerry went several times to a psychologist, Susan, and she gave up telling Jerry this was an unusual, unexplainable situation that he had to live with.

TYPEWRITER MAN

Up to that time, everyone who wanted to make a gift to Jerry knew what to buy him -- another electric typewriter.

While Jerry was on a weeklong business trip, his wife Sally, with the aid of the children donated all 37 typewriters to a charity except for one, his old Royal.

When Jerry returned, Sally had a new typewriter, a Brother for him. Sally said Jerry should no longer clutter his life with useless typewriters. She also told Jerry that he could join an online group which traded typewriters and he did so. He obtained a second Brother typewriter and he continued to utilize that online group trading in each time his then useless although operable typewriter after each one quit typing after his seventh new writing.

Thereafter, Jerry lived happily with his family. Jerry never self published or otherwise ever published any of his writings or short stories.

LARRY'S LAST CHRISTMAS

Larry was 51 years old when he died. Larry at the time of his death had been married for 23 years to Alberta, and they had four children, Kate, 20; Sam, 18; Joe, 14; and Amy, 12.

Larry was a pharmacist at Giant Eagle and the family was financially secure. Alberta worked part time as a dental assistant. Kate was in her third year at college and was changing her major from political science to Pre-pharmacy. Sam was in his first year at college with a planned major in criminal justice.

It was the last day before Christmas and everyone was home.

Larry reluctantly celebrated Christmas for the sake of the children. He had always believed that too much was made of this Holiday and the gift giving was excessive.

Four years prior, Larry and Alberta made a pact to restrict their gift giving for each other to one gift at Christmas and likewise at their birthdays and their anniversary. They lived up to that decision but could not stop themselves from buying and giving too many presents to the children. Larry knew he was a benevolent hypocrite but accepted this fault. Larry often brought home for Alberta minor gifts just because such as flowers; donuts; cream puffs etc. even though he was on a constant diet and claimed to swear off sweets and deserts. He succeeded to some extent and had shed six pounds in the last three months. Larry knew that the Christmas holidays were his waterloo since his Aunt Doris would provide her irresistible fudge; cousin Tammy her éclairs; and he could not talk Alberta and the children from making seemingly endless quantities of homemade ice cream -- vanilla -- cherry -- chocolate delight (don't ask for the recipe) and each Christmas they tried a new decadent flavor.

This afternoon, Larry had easily succumbed after tasting just one tablespoon of their latest concoction -- Strawberry ice cream with layers of caramel and dark chocolate interlaced.

LARRY'S LAST CHRISTMAS

Larry while eating or inhaling a large bowl, kept remonstrating that they should quit tempting him.

That last afternoon was spent eating and playing board games. Larry finally won both games of checkers from Joe and a very surprising win at chess from Kate.

At four o'clock p.m. Larry kissed Alberta and said he would go and get her two cartons of cigarettes knowing she was almost out and even though Larry had never smoked he knew that Alberta could not quit until she wanted to. Larry was aware he was enabling Alberta but believed she would get cigarettes anyway and it was a small matter for him to run that errand.

The streets were snow and ice covered but Larry arrived at the store and bought the two cartons.

In the adjoining street as Larry was placing the cigarettes in his car, there was a terrible crash.

Larry ran out into the street and helped to get the woman driver and her two children out of her damaged vehicle. They were not severely injured. The woman said, "I need my purse - it has the inhaler for my son and he is starting to have an attack." Larry said he would retrieve her purse and as he did so and was handing it to her, another vehicle came around the corner and lost control striking the two cars which were in the middle of the road and caromed off hitting Larry. Larry died at the scene the way he had lived all of his life, helping others.

Indirectly, Larry saved the life of his beloved wife, Alberta, since her guilt in having Larry in his last moments of life spent going out and buying cigarettes for her caused her to quit smoking. When she saw a doctor a few months later, the doctor told her that by quitting when she did saved her life.

Two of the children, Kate and Joe who had commenced smoking both quit also and never smoked again for their lifetimes.

Larry had helped the lives of the mother and two children who might have died in the second crash and he also saved the lives of Alberta, Kate, and Joe.

FIRST THANKSGIVING FOR RITA AND ED

Rita, age six and her brother, Ed, almost five, had been in the foster parent system as long as they remembered. They have no knowledge of their birth parents. That morning Rita was telling Ed that this is the fifth foster home.

It was early November and they were strapped in their car seats and Molly was driving. They had been with Molly and Tim, her husband since July and they were looking forward to their very first Thanksgiving in a house and not at an institution.

Molly swerved to avoid hitting a small animal and crashed her car into a tree off the road.

Molly suffered a badly injured neck. Rita had ribs injured and a broken left arm. Ed had many bruises. They all ended up at the same hospital. Tim came at once. Molly needed special rehab and Tim talked to the foster parent caseworker, Tammie. It was decided that a new temporary foster home would have to be secured for Rita and Tim.

Nanci and her husband, Jim, had recently volunteered to be temporary foster parents and were certified.

They have been married for nine years and Nancy had had four miscarriages and their doctor, George told them not to try pregnancy ever again since the life of Nanci would be in serious life-threatening danger. The last miscarriage occurred more than a year ago.

Jim and Nanci had discussed adoption but basically ruled this option out.

They had enrolled and were successful in being certified as foster parents. Tammie went to see Nanci and Jim and implored them to take in Rita and Ed telling them that Molly was expected to be fully recovered in early December and would with her husband Tim, resume being foster parents of Rita and Ed.

FIRST THANKSGIVING FOR RITA AND ED

Jim and Nanci agreed knowing it would be for less than two months. Tammie arranged for Rita and Ed's clothes, toys, and personal belongings to be delivered to the four-bedroom, two bath home of Nanci and Jim.

The next morning Jim and Nanci visited Rita and Ed in their recovery room. Rita and Ed were to be discharged the next day. Rita, with curly brown hair and intense brown eyes said to Ed "well, this makes the sixth foster home in three years." "Maybe, Molly will get well and we can be back with her and Tim for our first home Thanksgiving."

Jim spoke up "You will have a real Thanksgiving at your new home with Nanci and me."

Rita with a cast on her left arm and Ed still sore went to live with Nanci and Jim and this was three weeks before Thanksgiving. An evening three days before, Jim and Nanci discussed with Rita and Ed what they desired for their first Thanksgiving. Ed said, "We want Turkey and Ham -- mashed potatoes -- no cranberries but strawberries with milk also chocolate milk. I like Rye bread and Rita likes pumpernickel bread and for dessert- apple pie with vanilla ice cream." Rita agreed while Nanci went over each request and took notes.

On a crisp November day, Jim, Nanci, Rita and Ed sat down and eagerly enjoyed exactly as requested the first real home Thanksgiving dinner.

Over the three weeks that Rita and Ed had been with Nanci and Jim, a special bond had been created. In contrast to the other foster homes, this time they all were together every evening and weekends because Jim had his own successful business and Nanci enjoyed being at home. Nanci had been typing her life story so that she could express her sorrow regarding the miscarriages.

Sincere love and true affection abided in this home. Jim and Nanci talked about adopting Rita and Ed.

FIRST THANKSGIVING FOR RITA AND ED

Tammie called and came over to see all of them the day after the Thanksgiving feast and told them that Molly was not recovering and that she and Tim would not be able to resume foster parenting of Rita and Ed.

Nanci and Jim went to great lengths along with Rita and Ed explaining to Tammie that they were a real family and they wanted and needed each other so much that they would take every action to successfully adopt both children.

Tammie, having been frustrated by her failure to have Rita and Ed placed in a stable loving home till now agreed and said she would expedite the adoption process.

After Tammie left, Rita and Ed with one mutual voice said, "This has been our best first Thanksgiving. Now let us start planning the best ever first Christmas."

Nanci and Jim, laughing, agreed.

IMMIGRANT

Joseph, now 46, does not have a true memory of being brought to the United States when he was three years old. When alive his parents, Sam and Ruth, often related the tale of their troubled journey entering this country illegally. Sam and Ruth died a few years ago leaving Joseph an orphan. Joseph thinks there was a sister who died soon after birth. He may have relatives but is not aware of them.

Joseph did very well in school and excelled in Chemistry. He went to college and graduate school on full scholarships and majored in both molecular chemistry and quantum chemistry. Joseph knows he is not a citizen and has never voted.

Joseph married Isabel, a born U.S. citizen some 22 years ago and they have four children, Jackie, age 20, completing her third year of college studying physics and mathematics; Ronald, age 18, and finishing his first year at the university with a planned major in engineering; Samuel, age 16, who aspires to writing poetry; and Anna, age 14, whose main interest is pottery. Isabel is a painter of some renown and manages a non-profit dealing with immigration issues.

Joseph last year was short listed for the Nobel Prize in chemistry. He owns patents on chemical treatment using nano-sized chemical devices to hopefully cure some cancers. Joseph has been honored with well earned academic and world based awards. He is contracted to sell part of his patents if they prove out in human studies so that he will receive well over 100 million initially with royalties to be paid in the future.

Joseph was elated when President Obama issued an executive order barring deportation for children brought illegally into the U.S. but determined this did not apply to him since he was too old. Joseph fully approved the law passed by the U.S. Senate (but stalled in the House) which created a 13 year path to U.S. citizenship but was not interested in coming out as an illegal immigrant pursuant to such law. Joseph had never lied on any governmental or other form with regard to the question of being a citizen. Several times he turned down any federal position since his citizenship might be questioned.

IMMIGRANT

Joseph had and still has the option of emigrating to many other nations which would more than welcome him in the event that any serious effort was made to deport him.

Joseph always thought of himself as an American and he loved the United States and wanted to live out his life here.

Someone reported Joseph as an illegal immigrant to INS and legal action was initiated which could lead to his deportation. The country that he would be deported to wanted him to come there to live. Joseph did not enter any formal contest to the deportation Academia and the business community did so. This became a lasting media issue.

There was a proposed bill in Congress as has often been done known as a private bill or law in favor of one individual and in the case of Joseph would grant him retroactive citizenship. Joseph refused this legal remedy.

Joseph wrote an open piece stating he would accept instant U.S. citizenship if all other illegal immigrants who were brought to this country at 14 years of age or younger and who have in their lifetimes been good citizens would be treated the same.

The President did bar deportation for any person brought to this country when they were 14 or younger but his executive order would not grant any method for citizenship nor prevent a future administration from changing such executive order.

Tremendous political pressure occurred and the law originally called the "Dream Act" was enacted into law.

Authors Note: This is a fiction story and as of this date did not happen nor was the comprehensive immigration reform law allowed to be voted on in the House of Representatives.

TRUE LOVE

Roger was six when he fell hopelessly in love with Alicia, then five. Roger saw Alicia across the crowded playground. Alicia had golden hair and blue eyes and was vivacious and a daredevil. Alicia was there with her older sister and younger brother. Roger, with brown hair and brown eyes, was shy and rarely spoke.

Alicia's sister, Terrie, took their brother, Eli, to get ice cream. Alicia went up the longest slide even though it had a sign saying "Out of Order -- DANGER."

Roger saw what was about to happen and ran over and positioned himself where he believed Alicia would fall. Roger was right but did not realize how heavy a little girl was until he took the full force of Alicia's falling body, knocking him to the ground. Roger hit the back of his head and saw stars but he knew he was in love since he had cushioned Alicia who suffered no injury except where her nose hit his chin. Terri and Eli came running and Alicia was blamed for this ill-conceived adventure. Terry insisted on going home Roger still dazed on the ground heard a soft "thanks" and lips brushed his face.

Roger went to a different elementary school than Alicia so they rarely saw each other.

Roger kept a journal and he seldom made any entries except noting each time he had any encounter with Alicia.

During the next six years, Roger did see Alicia at the playground and other than saying "Hi" they seldom spoke and seldom spent time playing together.

A few times a year both Roger and Alicia would be at the same movie but they did not socialize there.

Roger believed that Alicia was too lovely for him and he kept his distance.

They did attend Middle and High School at the same time except that Roger was two years ahead of Alicia as he had advanced one extra grade and was also a year and two months older.

TRUE LOVE

The only memorable event occurred when Alicia went to the Senior-Junior spring dance. Alicia was with a burly baseball player, a junior named Syd, while Alicia was a sophomore and Roger was a senior who had taken his cousin to the dance. The cousin was also named Alicia and while dancing, Roger holding his cousin, daydreamed that he was dancing with his true love, Alicia. It was a clear evening in early May and Roger took a break and went outside. Roger saw Syd manhandle Alicia and tore her dress. Alicia cried out and Syd came to his senses and let her go.

Roger came up behind Syd and tripped Syd. As Syd lay on the ground, Roger straddled him and choked him. Just before losing consciousness, Syd heard in his left ear, "never hurt Alicia ever." Syd recovered and heeding that never went near Alicia.

Roger and Alicia took different paths in life. Roger moved away for several years pursuing his passion as a botanist and to find in faraway places unusual plants.

Roger came back to his hometown when he was 32.

Alicia, then 31, had a creative life as a still life artist using both photography and oil paints. Alicia had married Ken who for most of their three years together was drunk and abusive. Alicia had one miscarriage at three months when she was knocked down by Ken. Alicia was 23 when divorced and two years later she married William and she was still married to him when Roger came home to live.

The other Alicia, Roger's cousin, had become for several years the best friend of Alicia and they shared confidences.

The cousin Alicia was happily married and had a photographic career of note.

TRUE LOVE

Roger wanting to know about his true love received much information from his cousin. He was told that William would a few times a year fly into an unprovoked rage and physically abuse Alicia. Alicia had battered wife syndrome and did have two miscarriages and never made any attempt to leave William despite being at the hospital emergency room several times.

As related by his cousin, Roger was told that Alicia just the last evening had suffered a broken arm, a badly cut lip and severe bruising. She was to stay in the hospital for tests and rest for two days or more.

Roger thought and considered what to do for a few hours. He then went to the home of Alicia and William and entered the unlocked back door.

Roger found William n his bedroom nude and drunk. Roger woke William up and took him to the bathroom. Roger filled the bathtub and urged William to take a warm bath. William went in the bathtub and Roger drowned William.

More than 24 hours later William was found dead and all indications including an injury to his head and his level of intoxication with no evidence of forced entry all led the police ruling this was an accident.

Alicia received the considerable life insurance payment and inherited their joint assets and William's separate stock and bond portfolio.

During the next year the two Alicia's stayed close and Roger was reintroduced to Alicia. Alicia warmly welcomed Roger recalling the he saved her when she was five years old.

Roger buried deep his killing of William knowing that was the only way to again save Alicia.

Roger dated Alicia and on a cold December afternoon proposed to her and she said, "Sure."

And so it became a sure thing and they were happily married.

CRIMINAL BACTERIA

It is many years into the future and James, 14 years old is the first juvenile sentenced to have the criminal bacteria procedure.

James had been in the juvenile justice system since he was seven years old. Although he has yet to kill, he has come close.

James came to Court with a record of multiple assaults and armed robberies. James was designated an adult so that he could face trial and once convicted would be sentenced to life imprisonment with little chance for parole.

James had some redeeming features -- he had intelligence, scoring at about 130 on the standard IQ test; he was oddly soft spoken; and he was a major reading of books and magazines.

In conversation, James was knowledgeable regarding national and political issues. He was an avid movie goer and had seen a majority of the Academy Award films.

James had robbed many stores and stole old movies so that when finally caught he had a collection of over two thousand DVDs. James particularly liked black and white movies from the 1940s and 1930s.

If one conversed with James about those subjects, he was very articulate.

The science of transferring good bacteria into the brain area controlling emotions had rapidly grown and live persons were needed to study this matter.

It was decided to offer individuals like James -- young -- facing draconian sentences -- perhaps redeemable if this bacteria therapy works -- violent and aggressive but not yet killers.

James along with 99 others were told about this criminal bacteria test and offered the choice of life imprisonment or if this treatment was a success, they would be released in five years.

James asked, "Do I go free if after five years, this bacteria therapy does not work on me?" He was so assured and this became a legally binding contract.

CRIMINAL BACTERIA

All 100 agreed and the treatments were begun. This was not a blind study where say half were given a placebo. All received this bacteria infusion over several months. They were in a secure location where every move could be efficiently monitored.

During those five years, two committed suicide, one due to a serious but rare side effect of the infusion of the "good" bacteria. The other suicide was an erotic accident that went wrong and that 15 year old strangled himself.

About twenty or so had recurring side effects, including fatigue and dizziness. Most recovered with little problems. Three were released early form the trial test due to bleeding and acute nausea, other side effects.

95 completed the five year program. 60 of them including James based on intensive tests had their personalities changed dramatically so that basically all violent tendencies and aggressiveness disappeared. Their emotional disposition toward crime was gone. Unfortunately the remaining 35 still were violent, aggressive and seemingly addicted to criminal activities.

On the good side over 20 of those 35 were helped by the good bacteria therapy so that they moderated in large measure their criminal tendencies so that they did not again get charged for crimes during the next twenty years. The final 15 were kept under close supervision and within three years, 8 were convicted of serious crimes and imprisoned for twenty or more years. Three of the remaining seven were killed in police shootouts and two committed suicide. The final two vanished.

CRIMINAL BACTERIA

James did get a scholarship and went to college, with a major in both creative and professional writing. James had a book published being his memoir titled "A criminal life saved by good bacteria." It was a best seller and by the age of 24 James was in fact famous. He became a column writer re: national politics and on the side was a movie critic of note. When James was 27 he met courted and married Trudy, then 25, and a budding fashion designer and a hobby chef. James never did any criminal act. They had two children and adopted three others.

The landmark five year test and therapy regarding good bacteria was replicated all over the world resulting in a reduction of violent and aggressive crimes by well over 70%.

James was always proud that he had made the informed choice to have good bacteria infused into his brain.

PROCREATION FOR ROBOTS

It is the year 2075. In the United States and most of the world, robots are utilized in all endeavors. Robots have succeeded in securing the right to marry except in India, Kenya, South Africa, Guam, Bali, and France.

In those nations, any robotic attempt to marry is met with mandatory destruction. Whatever remains is shipped to a special place in outer Mongolia which has become the electronic dump site of the civilized world.

By this time 3D imaging manufacture is pervasive being in most homes and industry. Technology is embedded by mind in all 3D machines - GPS; owner identification; failsafe devices so that for example plastic weapons cannot be built. The 3D machines are programmed to totally self destruct if any attempt is made to do illegal and/or immoral actions with such machines. These devices are required worldwide and are stringently enforced. Any human trying to evade these devices and laws is banished for life until death on the penal colony on the moon.

Robot Z and Robot Q have been married for several years and are "happy." Except they both have the artificial emotions of love, caring, affection and have always desired child robots to complete their family. They could have "adopted" a robot but that was contrary to their feelings. They earnestly wanted to robots to educate and to be their descendants in the future and to carry forward the robotic dream of enchantment of artificial intelligence and freedom/democracy.

Both Z and Q have outlived their usefulness and are retired. In two years they will both go to what they call "The scrap yard in the sky" --- actually the scrap yard in outer Mongolia. They have fully accepted this end but want a legacy.

The female robot, Q is a skilled electronic and mechanical engineer and the male robot, Z, has studied artificial intelligence his entire life.

They have tinkered in their hidden workshop but without an advanced 3D machine they can go no further in "procreating" two robotic children.

PROCREATION FOR ROBOTS

Robot AIC who they knew quite well was scheduled to go to Outer Mongolia in a week and came by for a visit with Robots Q and Z. AIC had overwhelming implanted emotions of friendship and the feeling "to give is divine."

AIC told Q and Z about the grandfathered repository of 3D machines at Fort Knox; Pennsylvania, near Erie, Pa. and provided them with all needed clothes and official documents to take legal possession of three advanced 3D machines.

The next week after attending the planned eulogy for AIC, Q and Z rode their robotic transportation to take the robotic Railroad to its terminal located in Edinboro, Pa. (Erie County) on what has become well known as the former "Sometimes Raging Creek Farm" donated by the children of Joy Grieshober to improve the robotic lives of Robots worldwide. This land was preserved as originally intended and was donated in the year 2068 and the robotic RR terminal was then erected.

The driving forces behind this project were Elijah, Edy and Simon, grandchildren, and adopted grandchildren, Taylor III, John XX and John VV. (Readers -- ask for the writings re: Holly - John - Taylor - Elijah - Edy - Simon - Taylor III and John XX and VV.) (They are in books 11, 13, and 17 by the late Donald W. Grieshober -- those with the bright blue covers with gold or silver lettering).

Armed with their official documents and codes, Q and Z had no difficulty in obtaining three still functioning advanced 3D machines with all needed additional software, hardware and supplies. A large number of robots who revered Robot AIC helped load all these on the return Robotic RR car and Q and Z placed all three 3D machines in their hidden workroom.

For the next almost two years Q and Z worked diligently and "procreated" many robotic children. They decided to keep two named AV4 and TVA3 and provided all remaining robotic children "procreated" using the three 3D machines to various Universities, government agencies, and research and development facilities worldwide. Q and Z continued this secret endeavor aided by robots TVA3 and AV4.

PROCREATION FOR ROBOTS

Just before the two years were up, the other robotic children of Q and Z using their positions, skills, and knowledge cancelled permanently all termination of all robots.

This fiction story is only written until October 26, 2101 so at least till that date Q and Z and AV4 and TVA 3 were "procreating" robotic children.

IMPLANTS

When the wish, need or want first occurred, Josh was 14 and his older sister, Anita, was 16.

For some time Anita had deplored her small breasts. Where other friends, relatives and school foes were naturally acquiring curvaceous relatively large breasts, Anita was left behind. She was constantly lectured by her parents and others that bra size was of no importance. One of the favorite statements was, "Any young man who only sees your lack of large breasts to not want to be with you is a worthless person."

Anita's brain sort of accepted this concept but when repeatedly attractive young men passed by Anita and chose others based, she believed, primarily on curves and breasts with legs thrown in, Anita became increasingly depressed. She cared little for school or sports and school activities. She did not attend school dances and firmly believed that life was passing her by.

Anita was placed on antidepressant medications but those were of little help. Her parents, Tim and Jane, knew the solution -- provide Anita with breast enhancement but for one year they resisted this idea.

Shortly after Anita's 17th birthday she was rushed to a hospital since she took an overdose of the prescription pills. She left a letter of despair for her parents.

Tim and Jane, finally realizing the seriousness of the situation and finally concluding that Anita will be an adult in one year and that it was her life agreed and Anita had her breast enlargement operation.

Success was apparent and Anita having regained her needed self-confidence once again became a very good student. She attracted several young men and although she attributed those romantic overtures to her body shape and breasts she failed to give due credit to the fact that she had a distinctive personality and was a real pleasure to be around. The lucky fellow Chad who became her regular date in high school achieved the envied goal of dating a very personable young woman.

IMPLANTS

Rationally Anita matured as most people do and internally acknowledged that her whole package of personality and intelligence was far more important that her face, breasts, and looks.

In the meanwhile Josh was growing up and doing well in school. He was a good athlete, running the mile in track on the team and doing passably well in the high jump. In addition he was on the Tennis team and was an avid bowler. His passion was computers and video games and he was among the very few best at those endeavors. He invented at age 16 a universal remote device which could also control video games - TV - and computers. He obtained several patents and licensed this technology receiving in the first year over two million with the future royalties basically without limit.

Josh remained comfortable and unchanged in his attitudes and personality. However Josh became obsessed with the idea regarding having a miniaturized version of his invention implanted in his left shoulder area so that he would always have his device available and useable.

Tim and Jane were worn down by this obsession of Josh and though opposed initially finally agreed.

Josh had a successful implant operation and presumably Josh was the first and only person to have such a device implanted.

Josh went forward with his life becoming a true expert in inventing devices to fully control all electronic devices. He went into partnership with Microsoft since he admired and respected Bill Gates both as a person and for his visionary charitable worldwide endeavors. Both Microsoft and Josh prospered.

Josh and Anita often discussed how similar was their personalities and their "obsession" re: implants.

ELEVATOR TO NOWHERE

Jack was 31, an actuary, and for some time knew he had little to live for. Jack married when he was 27 and had actual memory of less than two years of happiness. This ended on a cold wintery day in February when his wife, Jackie, then 26 told him in no uncertain way that she was not bringing any child into this world and never with Jack. Jackie packed up one suitcase and told Jack she was leaving with Richard and Leon, and they were going to live together as a threesome. In her cruelty she showed Jack several photos of herself with Leon and Richard all nude. Jack was informed this cozy threesome was going on for over a year.

Jackie told Jack to get a divorce if he wanted one and she had arranged for a moving company to pick up her other belongings the next day.

That night, not able to keep the lurid images out of his mind, he had the first of many recurring thoughts to end his life. For the next two years suicide became a profound narrative that he barely could contain.

Jack functioned well at his employment and performed well. His habit was to come home - prepare a microwave meal - drink a small glass of red wine - watch TV without paying much attention and doing crossword puzzles. By doing so he had at least a mental life.

Jack studied and considered suicide by hanging himself; stepping in front of a moving train; jumping from a tall building; and ingesting prescription pills. His fear was that he would not succeed and end up a cripple.

Jack had the random thought of finding Jackie, Richard and Leon and killing them but his real fear of getting caught and going to prison banished that idea.

Jack, one evening, picked up an obscure magazine called "Weird Ends" and in scanning through found an ad that read as follows:

"A unique way to kill oneself -- take the elevator to Nowhere." "For $1,500.00 you can have the ride of your life and choose to die."

There was a cell phone number and Jack called. Jack was told to send half - $750.00 to a P.O box and he would receive directions to the location of the elevator.

ELEVATOR TO NOWHERE

Jack was advised to bring a small suitcase with one set of underwear -- pair of shoes -- his favorite shirt -- three pens, blue, black, and red ink ones -- notebook; and comfort food and drink to last exactly four days. Jack was instructed to sell or give away all his assets and possessions and to make his last will and testament. Per advice he resigned from his job and wrote final letters to any of his relatives and friends that he wanted or needed to communicate with.

When Jack arrived at the elevator he was asked if he wanted to go solo or to be with other strangers on his last journey. He decided to go alone and was placed in elevator 13x. Once inside the elevator was locked -- it was plushy and had a bed and two chairs and was well lit. It had no buttons up or down and was fully automatic. Jack could and did dial up old shows and new ones on the preprogrammed TV. There was no news nor weather report.

Jack had chosen the option of going to sleep on the fourth night and not wake up. Jack had made arrangements to be cremated. Jack was also given the option of stopping his suicide by saying three times, "I want to live."

The elevator, as programmed, went at various speeds endlessly up and down.

Jack, using the inked pens, wrote his story and watched reruns of Gunsmoke -- Mash -- All in the Family and his favorite -- Bosom Buddies. Jack also saw Gone with the Wind – Gravity-- Ben Hur -- Its a Wonderful Life -- Its a Mad Mad Mad Mad World -- A Funny Thing Happened on the Way to the Forum. He saw plays including -- West Side Story -- Pygmalion -- and others.

Jack ate and savored each meal. Jack sort of got used to the repetitive motion of the elevator. He slept for eight hours each night. He contemplated his life and was completely convinced that he had made the right choice in using the elevator to nowhere as the method to end his life. Having eaten all the food he had and taken his last drink Jack went to sleep with inner peace on his mind. Jack died before morning and was cremated. He was clutching the book - "To Kill a Mockingbird."

ELEVATOR TO NOWHERE

The elevator to nowhere still exists and is in continual use. For those who do not want to use the elevator to nowhere they have innumerable ways to accomplish what Jack did.

TIGHTENING BELT

For years too many to count there has been a serious problem for men of all ages and for some women. The problem--how to keep trousers or pants up around the waist. There was the suspender solution. For some cultures, i.e. Muslims, the solution was to wear dresses and no pants.

For the vast majority, one had to constantly hitch up pants and/or tighten a belt. Too often to count, how many times did pants fall down to resulting humiliation, embarrassment, and laughter?

In a country far away a new solution was invented, the automatic tightening belt. This remarkable belt had built in sensors so that the belt would automatically tighten and loosen throughout the time period of wearing pants and a belt.

In the first two years over a billion belts called "the only belt" and men and some women were ecstatic.

However, a scientist named Franklin invented another use for this tightening belt. In the same country laws were passed requiring upon conviction that malicious liars would be compelled to wear the "tightening belt" for two years. At the end of two years if no further malicious lies was told by the wearer then the penalty would stop. If the wearer told even one malicious, hurtful lie then the belt would automatically tighten so that the wearer liar would suffer from such belt. This tightening belt could determine the extent of vicious punishable lies and act accordingly. After a period of time usually a month the belt would loosen and go back to normal.

Over time a few wearers died from the tightening because they were chronic repeating malicious liars.

Within a short period of time people kept their malicious thoughts of lying unspoken and a more civilized community came to exist. Anyone convicted of lying about another person being a malicious liar was sentenced to also wear the tightening belt.

TIGHTENING BELT

The company that Franklin worked at was busy developing other uses for the "tightening belt" such as for shoplifters -- the belt would automatically tighten if a new shoplifting offence occurred. Similarly for public drunkenness -- ranting and raving in public -- serious disturbing of the peace -- using vile and obscene in public words.

Several other countries used this belt to quell protestors who persisted in assembling in opposition to the government.

Criminal elements found ways to use this belt to control their minions. Some factories required the wearing of the belt while working so that if a worker wearer slacked off or abused equipment or did not work efficiently the belt would tighten.

Parents used the belt on rebellious teens. Many cases of parental abuse were brought against parents misusing the belt. College students used the belt illegally to hurt fellow students such as hazing. Rumors were wide spread of sexual use of the tightening belt. There were successful prosecutions of killings using the belt as the murder weapon. Also this became a major suicide since if the belt tightens enough the wearer lost consciousness and died of internal organ strangulation.

What was one of the best inventions regarding the quality of life was used in unintended ways and sometimes for evil.

Of course this has always been true in history -- for example electricity is used for good and yet causes death and injury. Cars are used for good actions but speed kills. The 3D imaging machine is proudly beneficial but can be used for evil by creating the plastic pistol.

Once the genie is out of Pandora's box it cannot be returned and only wise humans can lessen the evil acts that good, useful inventions can be used for.

BRAIN DAMAGED--PREDICT FUTURE

In the United States many people suffer traumatic brain injuries and damage. A graduate student, Alice, at a University was compiling information re: a PHD thesis and came across scattered news stories about women aged in their early thirties who had serious brain damage and for five minutes once a month made predictions about the future. This was considered an aberration and was given scant acknowledgement.

The student, Alice, found five such women in her area and decided to do her PHD thesis using them to determine the validity and accuracy of their future predictions. Alice, after much effort secured permission to talk to these five women, Audrey; Josie: Hester: Marie; and Sybil. Alice did over several months conduct intensive interviews and found that those five women had many common traits. The all had attended college and had BAs in science--all had promising careers--all were involved in automobile accidents--all had similar near death experiences--all were recovering from their injuries--all were married for six years--all had two children, a boy aged five and a girl aged three. None of them were acquainted in any manner with one another. Each described in precise detail the same semi dream which then was at once followed by a trance in which they each predicted for the first time some future event. They never communicated with the others. Most strange was that each had their initial prediction trance on May 15th at 3:36 p.m. All Five recounted the exact predictions they uttered and every future prediction came to be true in every detail.

Even stranger was the fact that all five could only be in this prediction trance for five minutes, no more and no less.

Further these episodes all occurred at 3:36 p.m. on and only on the fifteenth of each month except for July, the month that each had suffered brain damage.

BRAIN DAMAGED--PREDICT FUTURE

It took Alice seven months to write her PHD thesis and it was published and republished in psychology prestigious journals. Alice with the permission of all five also wrote a best seller which became a worldwide sensation. Many people tried to debunk this phenomenon but to no avail. A TV special for two hours in prime time was produced live with Alice presenting her version. Then Audrey; Josie: Hester: Marie: and Sybil; for precisely five minutes each did their future predictions. A one and a half hour special occurred six months later recounting that each one accurately predicted future events. For a half hour before there was a repeat of the future predictions of each of the five women.

Following those two television shows none of the five had the ability to ever predict the future again.

Alice for a few years was on the prestige lecture circuit. Alice became famous from these events and lived a very good life.

Alice married Dan and she likewise had a boy and a girl. Alice and the five, now fully recovered from brain damage, women met for combined family outings several times a year. With the help of Alice each had written a memoir detailing their lives and restating for history the various future predictions each had made during the three years that they had what was called "the exactly five minute trance and the resulting true future predictions."

KISS BUSINESS

Everyone needs different hugs to ease sorrow - when one does something good -- when a tragedy occurs -- sometimes just because and of course for romance and love.

The same thing regarding kisses with one added dimension, that is, a real sexual element. Often a kiss is accompanied by hugging. Dave and Michelle decided to open a business to be called simply "kisses and hugs."

Dave and Michelle were both 26 and were reaching the end of regular unemployment compensation and both had no success in finding a job.

They converted a garage at Dave's parents' home and printed out advertising flyers reading:

Grand Opening

Hugs and Kisses -- what ever you need or desire.

15 minutes for $45.00. No clothing removed

Anyone needing a hug or a kiss is welcome. No erotic moves allowed. Tipping is permitted.

Be the first ones to enjoy the solace and comfort of a caring person. There are no guarantees in life and therefore none regarding hugs and kisses.

The first day- six people came in, 4 men and 2 women. Dave and Michelle handled these customers. The two women were in their late forties and had lost their father recently. Dave provided a hugging session and did kiss each separately. They left feeling better about themselves.

KISS BUSINESS

One fellow in his twenties had just broken up with his girlfriend and wanted to test the waters by having a kiss and hug session which Michelle provided. One fellow thought of himself as God's gift to women and considered Michelle as fair game. Michelle gave him a knee where the sun does not shine and he was escorted out bent over. Everyone entering signed an application which clearly set forth this hug and kiss matter was for comfort purposes only and no eroticism was permitted. The other two men were in need of hugs primarily, one because he had lost his job, and the other had to have his favorite pet, a cat named Fluffy put down.

Due to the ads and word of mouth, this business flourished and soon Dave and Michelle hired two women and one man after serious interviews.

They secured all necessary licenses and permits and withstood a welcomed investigation as to whether or not any sexual activity was engaged in. Dave and Michelle along with their employees convinced everyone that their primary purpose was to provide a service of solace and comfort by the method of individual customized hugs and kisses.

Within a year Michelle met and married a customer, Roger. Dave needing comfort asked Danielle, an employee for a hug and kiss session and she readily complied. The hugging part felt good but when they kissed both Danielle and Dave knew that each was the one they had been seeking. They also married and Danielle retired since she only wanted to share her hugs and kisses with Dave and he agreed wholeheartedly.

ARROW AND ZESTFUL

June had been a hunter since she was five years old. There had been three hunters in her immediate family but two years ago, her sister, Anne, a little over year older, 20, died during bow and arrow hunting season when an arrow pierced her right leg and since she was hunting alone bled to death while stumbling and crawling through the woods. Anne was found by June and their younger brother, Sam, and they could not save her. Anne died zestful to the end and near her end had June and Sam pledged that they would carry on in hunting and to find the hunter who killed her.

June and Sam did hunt the next year but did not find any deer or other small game to kill but instead methodically searched the woods each day to find the killer of Anne.

They had the arrow as their clue and had found in an internet search that the arrow was a specialty arrow and was sold by a national chain of sporting goods stores. Only one of the stores was located in a forty mile radius of their home.

June had a list of eight individuals, 6 men and 2 women who purchased and used that arrow brand. Sam had discovered that two of the men had not been in these woods the year of Anne's death. One other man was injured on the first day of that hunting season and had not had the chance to use an arrow that year.

One of the women was actually on her honeymoon that bow and arrow hunting season.

In that first year after the death of Anne, June and Sam narrowed the possible killer to Roger, 35 years old and an expert hunter; Ruth, 33, mother of two, and who had tried out twice for the Olympics without success; Jim, 49, who was acknowledged to be the best hunter with a bow and arrow and who always within the first few days had a deer kill; and Bruce, age 27, who had been on his first hunt that year.

ARROW AND ZESTFUL

All four used the specialty arrow. Sam and June with the aid of a forensic expert, Sandra, had determined both the path and distance that the deadly arrow had taken that fateful day. They knew that the killer was about 125 yards away and that the arrow they believed had been aimed at a deer. It was zestfully surmised that there was a close miss of the deer and the arrow proceeded in a slightly downward path until it went into the right thigh of Anne and remained embedded there.

The coroner determined that Anne spent an agonizing almost three hours bleeding out while she tried to find help.

About a week before the current bow and arrow season, June and Sam decided to interview the four suspects, Roger, Ruth, Jim and Bruce. They were open with each stating why they were talking to them. It was found that Jim was not in or remotely close to the area where the killer had launched the kill arrow and he was eliminated. Ruth and Roger said they knew that area and might have been there but each stated they accounted for all their arrows and even showed Sam and June them. June and Sam did not eliminate Roger and Ruth since they easily could have replaced the arrow. Ruth in looking at the death arrow, showed June a curious mark on the shaft--a three dotted triangle which June had initially thought was a blemish.

Roger and Ruth allowed June and Sam to examine their arrows and no man made mark was found.

Sam talked to Brian, a friend of Bruce and Brian told Sam that Bruce being new to the bow and arrow hunt had marked his arrows so that if he lost one or more could have a means to identify and claim them. Brian also said that Bruce had a half dozen arrows so marked and claimed to lose four and said he had found two of them leaving two missing. Also Bruce had not gone hunting with his bow and arrows since that fateful year.

June and Sam confronted Bruce and asked him if the arrow they had was one of the two still missing arrows. Bruce found the marking and said this was one of the arrows he owned.

ARROW AND ZESTFUL

June with tears in her eyes told Bruce his missing arrow had killed her sister Anne. Bruce confessed that on that day he missed a deer and he did look for the missing arrow but did not find it. Bruce said he was disoriented with regard to the direction the missing arrow went and after a little while he gave up the search. Bruce asserted that he never saw Anne and never was aware that another hunter was wounded.

Brue was vague on why after that fateful day he never hunted again. He expressed remorse but stood fast in denying that he played any part in the death of Anne.

The District Attorney was contacted and made the decision to neither undertake an investigation nor to charge Bruce. His rationale was that firing an arrow in the woods and missing a deer and having his arrow strike another hunter was not a criminal act nor grossly negligent. Also that Bruce was not criminally liable for failure to properly search for the arrow. The DA, Henry, told Sam and June that they might succeed in suing Bruce for the wrongful death of Anne.

June and Sam did hire Andrew an experienced litigation attorney and after a year settled the lawsuit for $300,000.00. They used the amount after deducting the appropriate attorney fees and costs to fund education for novice bow and arrow hunters on their proper use.

A DRONE FOR XMAS

Jerry, 43, was happily married to Beth, 41. There were two children, Barbara, age 13, and Donald, age 12. Jerry had recently won a regional lottery and six weeks before Christmas, he had received $645,000 net after taxes. They paid some bills and saved equally $250,000 for retirement and $250,000 for education.

They had about $70,000 remaining and were trying to think what to spend this windfall on. Both Jerry and Beth worked for a software company for several years and were financially secure.

Beth had the habit of reading in bed before sleeping for usually an hour. Beth was eclectic and would read a book, newspaper, or a magazine. That evening she was reading a magazine and gave a shout to Jerry who was brushing his teeth fulfilling his ritual of brushing, flossing, and water picking his teeth three times every day. Jerry responded and Beth showed him the ad--The Pentagon was selling used refurbished drones stripped of all weapons, but with cameras etc. In four days there was to be an auction of 24 drones, small ones used for surveillance and larger ones which had capability of raining down death and destruction. They were all flyable but did not have advanced electronics. The successful bidder would also receive five hours of instruction in flying and maneuvering the drone purchased.

Jerry said "what a great family present for Xmas we have room in the extra garage. Both our children will love this gift. We have 11 acres here so we would not be causing any difficulty."

They successfully bought two drones, a small one and a large one. They told the children and all four participated in the instruction sessions.

A few weeks before Christmas they took turns flying the two drones. The local media, newspaper, radio, and television ran stories and videos of the family drones.

Two neighbors, Ralph and Joyce, picketed with others at their home carrying signs reading "Drones for dummies"--"Be lazy--have a drone do your work" "No residential drones."

A DRONE FOR XMAS

Beth placed an ad in the newspaper explaining the peaceful uses for drones and talking about her family enjoying life by being together flying the drones. She ended with the remark "Quit being a drone and a parasite, Come fly a drone."

The neighbors were invited by way of this newspaper article to come to their home on the Saturday before Christmas to fly the drones. Over a hundred came including about 50 children. Everyone had the chance to control and fly the two drones. There were three near misses where the drones almost collided. At some expense Jerry had collision and liability insurance regarding the drones.

On Christmas morning, a car came speeding up their driveway. Two neighbors, Jim and Alice, stridently said their daughter, Alicia, age four had wandered into the woods and a search was started. Alice begged Jerry and Beth to use the drones to search the woods. Each of the drones had some surveillance equipment and capability. Jerry and Beth agreed and with help loaded the drones on a truck. The drones were launched from a clearing and separately were operated by each Jerry and Beth. Barbara and Donald manned the computer screens to determine the location of the drones.

Within one hour the small drone had zeroed onto a still form partially hidden behind a large log. The drone hovered until a group of researchers arrived and Alicia was found. She had fallen and struck her head. Alicia was brought out to the waiting ambulance and sped to the local hospital. In three days, Alicia had basically recovered. The early discovery of Alicia may have saved her life but certainly helped her to recover sooner.

Jerry always praised Beth for reading the drone auction ad and often joined Beth in her habit of reading in bed before going to sleep.

The whole family celebrated the arrival of drones into their lives. Jerry during the summer bought two more drones so that each had one.

MAUD LOVES COMMERCIALS

Maud, now 44, a perennial housewife, mother of four, found her passion some three years ago.

Maud had to watch television since her husband, George liked sports and especially golf and tennis. To spend some quality time together, Maud had to watch to some extent these sports. She actually came to enjoy football.

The children from infancy each had television as an electronic babysitter. Maud and on occasion George would read books and excerpts from magazines to their children, Jane, now 15; Robert, age 13; Teddy, age 11; and Ariel, age 8. They all did well in school and with the exception of Robert, enjoyed reading. They were by and large a happy family. George was a CPA specializing in corporate federal income tax and arcane tax shelters. George also taught at the local university, teaching a course on federal and state income taxation.

Maud was a superb cook and did quilting. Mad was the driver of choice transporting the children to various sports and other activities. Maud volunteered at a soup kitchen twice a week and never missed any school activity. Maud was also able to play tennis year around and enjoyed the social aspect, the competition, and the exercise regimen.

If cookies, pies, or cakes are needed for any occasion, Maud was the one sought out to provide them.

Maud, about three years before, started to love commercials. Maud taped several programs and then spent about an hour per day deleting the shows and only watching the commercials.

Maud spent time compiling a journal where she kept a record of commercials and had her special rating system.

MAUD LOVES COMMERCIALS

Maud found the way to create a visual album of only commercials. If Maud learned that a friend, neighbor, or relative had any interest in viewing commercials, she produced her collection and would regale the guest with her commentary on commercials. Maud went on their high speed internet and researched commercials. George and the children had no problem in selecting presents for Maud since they found books and other material on her favorite hobby and passion--viewing and studying commercials.

Maud, in the past year, developed a blog and twice daily posted comments and reviews of commercials. Three months ago, Maud went commercial regarding television commercials and was earning over $5,000.00 per month from this business.

Maud was approached to write a book about the history and growth of commercials and she has agreed to do so.

In order to make time for her blog and the book, Maud has simplified her life and has become a true time expert. George and the children have been supportive of Maud loving commercials. Teddy and Ariel have been eager assistants and will be acknowledged for their help in the book.

The title of the blog is "Maud loves Commercials." This is also the initial title of the book but the publisher and Editor will have the final say.

Maud and the family are happy that Maud has a vibrant passion. Secretly each has come to like commercials.

BOUNTY AND YOUTHFUL

Jack was 19 when he had a bounty placed on his capture. Jack had a juvenile record starting when he was 15 and broke some windows. He was not placed in the system and spent as few as two different days and nights in jail.

Jack about six months before ran afoul of the law when he joined what were two peaceful protest demonstrations. One was a female driven protest about the imprisonment of a black woman in Georgia for what appears to be a typical southern miscarriage of justice. The protestors, including Jack, blocked access to the regional Federal courthouse. Jack did not act violently but was arrested for "disturbance of the peace" and a federal offence "Blocking and preventing justice." Jack refused advice to ask for a jury trial and he pled guilty along with others and paid a fine. By doing so, Jack acquired both a State and a Federal record.

There was a computer snafu and Jack was listed as not timely paying the fine (although he had a receipt showing payment) and a warrant was issued for Jack's arrest.

Several weeks later Jack joined another protest, this one by animal advocates protesting the extremely lenient handling of a woman who had multiple number of both cats and dogs dead or dying in her house.

This protest became somewhat violent and the police used teargas and flexible batons to quell this. Jack had not participated in the violence but was in the midst of being arrested. That day Jack had received a letter stating a warrant had been issued for his arrest for failure to pay the fine. Despite this clear warning Jack joined the public protest.

Jack had a good reason to participate in the three protests and her name was Taylor, a vivacious redhead, 20, and a junior at the University with a major in criminal justice.

BOUNTY AND YOUTHFUL

Jack met Taylor when he went to the University for information regarding taking adult education courses. Jack had a regular job at a book warehouse but believed that education was essential for his future. Jack was 6 foot tall and in good shape since he ran about three miles each day and played playground basketball. What attracted Taylor was obviously Jack being handsome and his speech pattern. Jack was a kind person and was constantly reading to self-educate himself.

Taylor was pretty and tall, 5 foot 9 inches, and was a fervent feminist. Taylor knew that Jack favored the feminine side of his personality. For six months Jack and Taylor had casual sporadic dates. Jack found a deep love of opera, not knowing its source, and they went to several operas and found a common liking for opera.

Taylor liked basketball and since Jack actually played that sport they found a shared feeling.

Where Jack and Taylor were truly alike was that they both enjoyed discourse in arguing different viewpoints pertaining to politics and national issues. Strangely enough, Jack was basically a conservative re: fiscal matters and personal responsibility but was moderate re: social issues. Taylor was a devout liberal democrat and espoused with vigor and determination her profound liberal views. Hence the peaceful protests which Jack willingly joined. Taylor was dismayed at Jack's troubles and felt guilty. Jack told her that he had in part caused his own difficulties and said he would go to the courthouse and the next day in effect turning himself in and using the official receipt to prove his innocence.

Both Taylor and Jack had some time previously jointly expressed the belief that though they had great affection for one another (neither had said out loud the words "I love you") they were neither ready to embrace a marriage commitment.

BOUNTY AND YOUTHFUL

Jack knowing he was in deep trouble ran from the demonstration. Another second warrant was issued or his arrest. Jack had given the official receipt to Taylor and she promised to employ an ACLU attorney to present Jack's case and she did so the next day. Perhaps because of her looks and demeanor Taylor was not arrested at the violent demonstration. It was claimed that Jack threw objects and broke store front windows. Taylor and three of her friends tried to explain that Jack did no such action but to no avail at the time the violence ended.

Jack therefore became a fugitive while the hired ACLU attorney, Fred, was making every effort to undo the damage. With some effort, Fred with the help of affidavits from Taylor and others established the innocence of Jack. But Jack did not know this and since this was one of many minor stories it drew zero media attention. Jack lost his job at the book warehouse.

Since initially Jack's bond of $12,000.00 was forfeited, a thirty five woman, Sally, who had a job as a bounty hunter was for some years assigned to find Jack and bring him to the authorities.

Another computer breakdown happened so that Sally was not informed that Jack was no longer a fugitive and all issues regarding his bond were cancelled.

Sally did find Jack where he was hiding and using mace subdued Jack and took him coughing and ill to the office of the federal magistrate. It was then learned that the youthful Jack had no bounty on him.

Sally left Jack there upon the arrival of both Fred, the ACLU attorney, and Taylor.

Sally muttered to herself "Another Stephanie Plum snafu" alluding to the fictional bounty hunter in the Janet Evanovich series of crime novels.

Taylor did give Jack a fierce hug and Jack reciprocated. As they left the courthouse Jack told Taylor "As much as I care for you I am giving up "peaceful" protesting."

CARES AND XANADU

Xanadu is a fictional abode and some people spend the better part of their life either seeking Xanadu or having unreasonable expectations and unrealizable dreams concerning this mythical place. In large measures this dream does no harm but allows such persons to spend their idle time and probably better use than trying to master video games (video games serve a useful purpose in improving eye and touch skills and maybe honing thinking skills).

John and Carrie, both in their mid twenties, who were casual lovers when in the mood or rather when one was in the mood even though the other was not, were consistent in their unreasonable dreams. They have been together in intimacy for about three years (although each has strayed for brief periods of time) and initially studied Eden and Paradise. Carrie had several discourse time periods with John and he was ultimately convinced that there was too much religious fervor in Eden and Paradise. For six months they casually studied off and on the concepts of Atlantis mythology; the truly utopian idea of Utopia. John insisted on ceasing any thinking about Utopia since it was futile.

For the past four months they have read and studied the nature of the word "Xanadu." To John, Xanadu was exotic and an unreachable location in the mists of time. For some unknown reason John started to equate Xanadu with The time warp of Brigadoon. The songs and enjoyment of the atmosphere of Brigadoon enthralled John. John actually sang many of the Brigadoon songs to Carrie. Carrie, on the other hand, desired to emulate CARRIE the creation of Stephen King, the horror novelist, and she built a scale model of Brigadoon and to the dismay of John on a midnight clear burned down the model. Carrie carried on by dancing a dervish dance around her destruction.

For John anything no matter how mad that Carrie did was a sexual turn on and they celebrated the destroying of Brigadoon by a sexual marathon lasting some eight hours two minutes and seventeen seconds. This episode tired out both Carrie and John and that was their mutual intent.

CARES AND XANADU

Brigadoon having become history and forgotten, two days later they started to study the concept of Xanadu. They cared for each other and to prove their caring nature they flipped a coin to decide who would go to the library, John, winning the toss and Carrie, to use the computer search engine Xavier (selected because both started with an X). Since they cared so much they utilized a two day--48 hour deadline--to produce all that could be learned about Xanadu. They were both literary writers so they each produced sixteen page double spaced on 50 lb paper a treatise on everything known or discoverable about Xanadu.

They cared so much they combined their research and self-published exactly 78 copies of a book which they titled "The non reality inexplicable mystery unsolved regarding the mythical and unknowable Xanadu."

The subtitle was "Seeking Xanadu."

Both Carrie and John went to several "readings" and soon they had a group calling themselves "Xanaduers," often at the readings that coterie dressed as though at Xanadu.

Carrie and John cared so much they decided to have a Xanadu wedding and it was well received. Their primary vow was to preserve at all costs Xanadu.

SPERM DONOR

Jack, then 22, became a sperm donor for the money. He passed all medical and psychological tests. Jack was tall, trim, had wavy brown hair and brown eyes with a small gold glint in them. Over the next year or so, Jack was chosen by 23 women (and their husbands) for artificial insemination.

Seven did not take at all. With regard to six conceptions occurred but within a few weeks after gestation started, all activity ceased and pregnancies stopped. The remaining ten did proceed normally until the sixth month. Eight miscarriages happened in the sixth month.. Two babies were born in their seventh month prematurely and were in a special nano medical unit.

During that year, the clinic was monitoring and testing to determine what was wrong with Jack's sperm. There had been no series of sperm disasters in the 23 year history of this AI clinic before. Two scientists who had been with the clinic for several years, Tim and Anita and were assigned to this task. Blood tests, MRI's, x-rays, DNA and other tests were conducted on Jack and the mothers involved. Samples were taken from the natural miscarriages to the extent possible. The two live babies in the nano unit were thoroughly examined. It took three months to find the cause. All of Jack's sperm at the clinic were destroyed.

A fierce debate ensued as to whether the clinic should reveal the result of this investigation and it was decided to avoid lawsuits and say nothing.

Jack was aware that something serious was wrong and he knew Carol from High School. Carol worked in the clinic office and she liked Jack. He had befriended her in her junior and senior years in high school. Carol did a computer search and printed out the report on Jack's sperm. Carol gave Jack the printout and Jack realized it would be tragic for him to father any children. The report stated that bacteria and enzymes in the sperm created near fatal allergy to the egg and would almost always cause a miscarriage.

SPERM DONOR

In the meanwhile the two live births were thriving and had no birth defects and went home. A further investigation determined that with regard to those two children, the mothers both violated protocol and had sexual intercourse with their husbands very near the time that Jack's sperm was used for artificial insemination. The basic theory was that the two sperm streams neutralized each other or that they merged in some unknown manner to in effect become one sperm.

When Jack learned this latest development and being aware that all 23 using his sperm produced no viable births he was devastated. Jack loved children and had a dream and desire to have biological children carrying on his genetic makeup and his DNA.

Jack took the only course he felt appropriate and had what was called an irreversible vasectomy.

Thereafter when Jack was in a good dating situation which to him was serious he told the women involved that he could not father children although he loved and desired children so that he would have a complete family life. Some of the women immediately ended their relationship with Jack but some others for a variety of reasons did not.

At age 28 Jack met, dated and courted Alicia, 27, a pharmacist, and told her his entire tale of woe. Alicia not only had profound sympathy for Jack but grew to love him.

Jack, now four years into his career as a stockbroker, felt real love for Alicia and he proposed to her.

Alicia said she wanted to say "yes" but needed to have an in depth discussion with Jack regarding children. Alicia expressed her deeply felt view that she wanted children for sure.

SPERM DONOR

Jack had investigated the adoption process in his state and believed this was not a viable option for them although if no other avenue happened he would reconsider adoption. Both ruled out just being foster parents. They discussed surrogacy where another woman would bear one or more children for them but Alicia ruled that out with logic stating that as far as she knew she could be fertile and pregnant and give birth to as many children as they both desired. The sensible method would be to use someone else's sperm. Jack at first resisted that method citing his situation as proof that this was not a good method. New and more complicated tests were available at clinics to test for and reject sperm donors.

Alicia and Jack could not decide if AI would work for them. They loved each other and decided to marry and give further thought to this matter later.

Two years after they married, the subject of children came up once again. They each had extended family and children from babies to toddlers to teens were at every family event. Jack overcame his reluctance and they used the most modern AI methods. Eleven months later Alicia gave birth to twin daughters, Jane and Hester. 14 months later AI was used again but when Alicia was four months pregnant, she miscarried. Jack believed this was a sign not to try again but Alicia disagreed thinking that her miscarriage was natural and in no way the result of AI procedures.

Alicia prevailed and about three years later Alicia gave birth for the second time to twins, this time boys named Roger and Richard.

Their family was now as complete as Jack and Alicia could ever want. The boys due to the AI selection resembled Jack and most people believed that Jack was their father. Of course in every aspect except for DNA Jack was their father and he displayed this attribute at all times.

Alicia since the births of Hester and Jane (actually five months earlier) had converted her career as a pharmacist to part time. Before the birth of Roger and Richard, she started working at home.

SPERM DONOR

Jack was doing very well in his stockbroker career but he knew that the happiness of Alicia depended on her continuing her chosen career.

Jack thought that being a sperm donor resulted in the worst situation he ever faced. But he also knew that he learned from being a sperm donor that without question he could never be a father biologically. However AI also produced for him and Alicia a wonderful family of four children. Jack came to the conclusion that as is true with regard to every aspect of human life, there are no black and white but only shades of gray. Jack accepted this and pledged to give no real time to any regret of his past and decided to fully accept the blessed result and to completely enjoy his life and family. And so it was.

LICENSED AND OPPOSED

Karen was opposed to Edward applying for a license to carry a concealed weapon. She believed that license would make Edward more vulnerable to violence. Edward had a career as an actuary and did not have any business reason to carry a concealed weapon. Edward told Karen he wanted to be armed and dangerous. Edward read western fiction and liked western movies. Edward collected old west items and had a room in his apartment which he called his "western room." He had hats, chaps, vests, spurs, boots, rifles, revolvers, holsters, and two western saddles. He had over 200 DVD western movies. He had bought all the old western TV series - - Gunsmoke - Rifleman - Wagon Train - Bonanza - Have Gun Will Travel - and many others.

At first Karen went along with this obsession of Edward but after 3 years together and the serial broken promises of Edward that he would propose, Karen reached the end of her patience. When Edward received his license and immediately put on the holster so he could have a concealed gun, Karen broke up with Edward.

About a week later Edward willingly went into a bad part of town (for the first time) late at night and proceeded to walk the streets as though he was a western lawman patrolling. Twice he stopped what he termed rowdy and wild behavior by pulling out his revolver and forcing the rowdy ones to run.

The third time Edward did this he was not so fortunate since two undercover police officers were present and arrested Edward. He pleaded guilty and was fined. His concealed weapon license was revoked. Edward tried to make up with Karen but she refused his efforts believing she had escaped a lifetime of misery. Karen knew that for her guns were in many instances needed but there should be reasonable regulations. When contemplating this entire situation she thought that Edward had an unstable personality.

LICENSED AND OPPOSED

Edward, now 34, met Annie, age 29, who was enamored of western culture and put Edward on a pedestal for his views and his western lifestyle and love of guns. Edward and Annie joined the NRA and supported that organization.

Edward was showing Annie one of the old rifles when it discharged hitting her in her left thigh. Annie recovered with a pronounced limp but felt so strong about Edward that she married him. One of their children, Abby, then four, was killed when the three year old, Robbie, picked up a revolver and shot her. Edward and Annie accepted this and maintained with no change their lifestyle.

Karen met Joseph when they both went to a gem show which also featured collectible rifles and pistols. They paid little attention to the weapons but both liked gems and they were drawn to one another. They had a lengthy conversation. At that time Karen had broken up with Edward some five months before and was in the mood for adventure and a new relationship with possible romance. Joseph, 30, felt his biological clock ticking and wanted to meet a woman with similar likes and values and to marry and have a family. Karen and Joseph clicked. Each believed that weapons were needed but had no obsessions regarding them. They had different views re: music but tolerated each other. They had similar tastes re: books, movies, television, etc. More profound was their mutual values about important issues: money -- children -- religion -- and to a lesser extent political and national matters They had certain biases but not deeply so. One example was that they both did not like excessive fat people but did have and enjoy friendships with people who had difficulty controlling their food intake. Neither smoked nor drank to excess.

Karen and Joseph realized they were kindred souls and within seven months they married. Karen was and continued to be a beauty consultant and Joseph was a midlevel manager. Financially there were no problems. Over the years, they had two children, Brigid and Theodore. There were no major tragedies in their lives and the family enjoyed regularly a happy family life.

MEDIOCRE AND NOXIOUS

Barry was about three weeks into 10th grade when he was labeled by a teacher, Anne, as "mediocre at best." This label stuck since Barry maintained a C average and never lived up to his potential. Barry showed slight interest in computer class but this did not last.

Barry was just under 6 feet tall and a lean 165 pounds when he received at the start of his senior year his second label. At this time Barry worked part time in a local chemical plant and the rancid smell of the chemicals he moved around clung to him. Barry approached a group of fellow students and they left him standing there even though he was only asking where the senior math class was located. They never responded but only held their noses and called out "you are noxious." This label stuck to Barry and this label among others were applied to Barry for a second reason. Barry had a very attractive wide and welcoming smile and bright twinkling blue eyes. He also had a golden hued wavy hair. Barry was a teen heartthrob and drew girls like a moth to a flame.

Barry played the dating field with a series of girls in 11th and 12th grades. Barry strangely enough wanted to date the intelligent girls and swept them off their feet. Barry was overly selective and would break up over relatively small matters such as a girl's view on gay marriage or global warming.

Several girls felt bad when these breakups occurred. They and their parents who were aware of these matters thought that Barry was a dangerous male and soon pinned him with the "noxious" label.

Barry after graduation for three years worked full time at the chemical plant. He dated a variety of young women who all believed their romantic situation with him was a dead end. Barry at that time was not interested in marriage nor any real commitment.

MEDIOCRE AND NOXIOUS

Barry during his time working at the chemical plant did retain the "noxious" label but soon discarded the "mediocre" label. Barry proved to be a devoted employee by never being tardy, willingly taking on difficult and sometimes dangerous tasks, and best of all displaying an avid curiosity regarding the mixing of chemicals.

Late in his third year with the company Barry experimented and discovered a new and profitable use for a chemical mixture unique to the industry. Barry was included at 10% with regard to the patent ownership.

Barry was promoted to the department of research and development and within another four years created several practical uses for his discovered chemical compounds. He became somewhat famous and very wealthy. Barry had shed the label "mediocre" for all time. Since he was in the R & D department and not dealing daily with chemicals, he also shed the label "noxious."

Barry soon acquired different labels -- smart -- successful -- energetic -- self taught -- handsome -- charismatic.

During those years Barry received well earned awards and acclaim. Barry was a fiscal conservative and did not splurge with his new found wealth. He bought a condo which was a wise investment. His only expensive purchase was his dream vehicle, a new dark blue Jaguar. The early year's electrical problems with the Jaguar automobile were in the past. Barry was also mechanically inclined and he kept that Jaguar for many years.

Barry when 32 embarked on an improbable mission -- to locate many of the high school girls he had in effect dumped and to some extent express his regret at his words and deeds. Barry expected nothing from this endeavor but felt a need to do so to ease his guilt feelings. Barry also thought by doing this journey to the past that he would then be free to have a committed present romantic relationship.

MEDIOCRE AND NOXIOUS

Barry had kept a journal which listed 14 names of girls so treated. He had help from a private detective, Dave, and found that one, Alicia had died in an accident. Three others, Trudy, Rose, and Betty, were married and Barry decided not to seek them out. Two others, Waverly and Tricia had moved far away and actually without a great deal of checking, were not discoverable.

That left eight. Barry had an encounter with Roberta, June, and Carol. They refused to accept they were "dumped" and rejected Barry's overtures.

Danielle was into illegal drugs heavily and at first did not recognize Barry. He intervened and got Danielle into rehab and this worked. Mary, when Barry contacted her had just had her latest breakup with her then boyfriend and was more interested in drinking her misery away than listening to Barry. Barry tried to help Mary but to no avail.

The final three, Fern, Grace, and Harriet, all were successful and had never married nor were they in any committed romantic relationship. Fern and Harriet agreed to meet Barry only together. This proved difficult since they both carried a lifelong grudge and spent the time berating Barry. After an hour of this venomous speech Barry left knowing that no matter what he said they were too involved in their unreasonable attitudes that no good would happen.

That left Grace and for a while Barry talked to her by phone since she was a traveling representative with a pharmaceutical company and quite successful. Barry persevered and invited Grace to dinner. They had an enjoyable dinner. Barry explained his acts and words to Grace and she at once said she had not forgotten that senior year episode but had long ago forgiven Barry. She reiterated that she at that time had an unreasonable attitude towards teen romances and was equally at fault.

MEDIOCRE AND NOXIOUS

They ended up going to a local tavern where they drank little but talked a lot. During their next three dates they both laid bare their lives and romances; their dreams and desires for the future. They soon learned enough about each other so that a meaningful committed relationship ensued.

Barry and Grace did marry and she moved into his condo and made what was an apartment into a loving home.

Grace continued her career and as she was promoted her travels became less and less. Barry created many patentable chemical compounds over the years.

Within four years Grace gave birth first to triplets, named Alice, Bernadette, and Chloe; and less than two years later, twin boys, named Jon and James.

Barry knew he had forever discarded the label "mediocre" and based on the sexual life and emotional love life he and Grace had, no longer would the label "noxious" apply.

WHAT IF PILL

Jennifer, now 31, unmarried, had a Master's degree in chemistry, and was working part time on a PHD degree. She had been employed in the R&D division of a small pharmaceutical company for eight years, starting when she was in her junior year of college.

She had sporadic feelings of lack of self-worth or self-confidence. She absorbed even mild praise for her work like an eager sponge. She was searching for a pill whether to be swallowed or chewed which would affect the brain and instill immediate self-worth even for a short period of time. Jennifer had written several theses on this problem believing that one of the prime causes of poverty is the individual belief of negative self-worth. Further if such person would believe in themselves even for a short time that ambition and perseverance could "kick in" and that person would start to lift themselves from future poverty.

Jennifer had studied the brain but was not an expert. Jennifer due to her negative attitudes was less than successful in her personal life. She thought she was in love several times and often thought she was way too easy with her emotions and willingly engaged in sex rather early in several relationships.

Jennifer in the eventual breakups was accused of being too needy for affection and too clingy. She also was probably bi-polar and often depressed. She believed that only a real confident man could save her but then concluded why such a paragon of confidence would want and need her. Would she end up in a marriage where she was the inferior one; the excessively needy clingy one, the truly non-confident one who has to have her ego and feelings massaged throughout life? Was she doomed to only be able to accept a loveless marriage of convenience?

She read many romantic books since they tended to depict independent confident women. She constantly read magazine articles meant to instill self-worth concepts.

WHAT IF PILL

The last breakup for Jennifer was three months ago and she had refrained deliberately from dating since. Jennifer's body shape resembled both Jennifer Garner and Scarlet Johannson so that she was attractive to many men. She had a rounded face with arched blond eyebrows, she was tall and curvy; her hair was a light blonde and since Jennifer was somewhat vain was always well done with various highlights. Her eyes were icy blue that seemed to light up and throw out a stream of sparkles when she was engaged in spirited conversation. She liked music, read different genres of books, and really liked movies. She had very strong views on current political issues but had learned to not express those unless she knew that she would not disturb those she was conversing with. She was a modest drinker but did not smoke nor indulge in illegal drugs. Several of the breakups occurred because the men acquired during their relations an excessive drinking problem or worse yet became a serious smoker of cigarettes. If Jennifer discovered that any man she was dating or considering to date downgraded women or displayed a profound macho personality, she ended that relationship.

Jennifer did have childhood memories of her parents. Sid and Doris, constantly ridiculing her or comparing her unfavorably to her two older brothers, Roger and Charles. She believed she was unfairly blamed for matters she did not do. In kindergarten, she simply retreated into solitude as a defense mechanism. She was not an unfriendly child in school but had to be pushed into activities. Up through high school she rarely volunteered in class but expressed accurately the answer when called upon. With no significant effort she excelled at school work and tests.

Jennifer early in life came to the conclusion she would be an introvert personality believing there would be less pain and misery. Many who would have welcomed Jennifer were soon put off by her defeatist personality.

WHAT IF PILL

She did not see much worth for her in sports except she did become through practice and effort a very good bowler. She usually bowled by herself. She joined in her senior year, a bowling team but put so much pressure on herself that she ended up with a good average of 182 but well below her ability. Again, feeling negative self-worth she did not bowl competitively again except once when she bowled in a three game tournament in a distant city which happened her junior year in college. She bowled two superb games of 212 and 223. Her negativeness kicked in and she only bowled 174 in the third game for a total of 609. She ended up winning $650.00 for her fifth place finish. Had she bowled 200 in this third game, she would have achieved first place.

Jennifer during her eight years at the company helped to discover many uses for drugs. She spent her free time working on the What If pill. Over the years she tried them on herself. In most instances, there was no affect as though she took an inoperable placebo. Once in a while a pill would give her a feeling of almost elation, or instill for the moment sadness or regret. None of her created pills instilled self-worth or confidence in her mind other than one pill which did for about ten minutes total. It made Jennifer feel so good that she thought she had found the "What If" pill. However, that pill seemed to be a calming peaceful pill and not one to create for example ambition and a work ethic. Jennifer kept that pill compound and made many efforts to combine its chemical component with others but to no avail.

Her discovery of that pill and its calming effect did alter Jennifer so thereafter she did personally feel more worthwhile.

WHAT IF PILL

David, 32, a fellow employee, pursued Jennifer. She started to date David and kept her negative feelings at bay in large measure so that David was actually seeing the real Jennifer as a confident independent opinionated woman. David's perception of Jennifer expressed in his words and actions coincided with her wishes for herself. When he proposed, she said yes, believing for the first time in her life that she could achieve a real goal, that of being a good wife and mother. The birth of three children, Tracy, Gertrude, and Timothy, solidified their marriage. Jennifer came to believe in herself as a wife and mother, and throughout her life and career made several memorable discoveries regarding pills and drugs and won awards, professional acclaim and earned wealth but despite her lifelong efforts never created the "What If" pill.

THE WAS NOT WEEK

Bruce, an acknowledged free lance artist, had his 29th birthday two months ago. He had a loft apartment with three bedrooms, one converted to his art studio and another to his professional artistic work. Although he dated some he was in no committed relationship and at this time did not want to be. Bruce usually went to sleep at 11:00 p.m. and woke up around 7:00 a.m.

This Sunday after looking at his calendar one more time, and noting two appointments, one at 10:00 a.m. to deliver the illustrated cover for a book and the other a noon luncheon to discuss an art project with three other artists, Bruce went through his usual routine and fell asleep.

Monday morning he awoke refreshed and ate a good breakfast. Since he had showered the night before he only did the minimum that morning. He had the television on but paid little attention to it. He planned to visit radio shack on his way to deliver and discuss the book cover so he went into his business bedroom. Bruce was astounded that all material regarding both the book cover project with Dave and the art project material to be discussed at lunch with Sara, Julie and Ray were missing.

Bruce searched all through his loft apartment with no success. He called Dave who at once asked Bruce why he is calling reminding Bruce the decision on the book cover would not be known until this coming Thursday but Dave reiterated that he believed it was the best cover Bruce had ever done and that he should not worry. After that conversation, Bruce thought he was losing his mind. Initially he thought Dave was playing a practical joke but Dave was all business on the phone.

THE WAS NOT WEEK

Bruce returned to his art bedroom and looked again at the landscape painting he was working on and saw it was almost finished. The last he remembered the painting was only partially done with much painting to be done on the seacoast and the sky area was just sketched in. Many thoughts went through Bruce's mind but no answers. He called Julie who he knew best and she immediately said to Bruce, "Wasn't that a wonderful productive luncheon last Monday with Sara and Ray?" Julie reminded Brue that they had an afternoon meeting on Wednesday at her apartment. Bruce holding his calendar saw that he had written
e meeting date and as also noted he had marked in Thursday with a "call Dave" notation.

Bruce looked at the calendar and saw he had a routine exam and cleaning with his dentist, Roger. Bruce called the dentist office planning to reschedule and was told that he did keep his prior appointment and scheduled a follow-up appointment in six months. Sure enough, Bruce had written on the calendar the next dentist visit.

Bruce received the morning newspaper but often did not read it in the morning. Bruce was amazed to see the Monday date and said to himself where did a week go? He watched TV and was again astounded to see that he had no memory of the "Was Not Week."

Bruce intensely reviewed the calendar and saw that he had other notations and made several calls finding out that he kept all appointments and performed all artistic endeavors as usual. He noted he had a blind date with Veronica set up by his cousin, Sue, and her husband Ted for dinner. Bruce first called Sue and she said that an enjoyable dinner had happened. Sue teased Bruce with the remark that what occurred when he took Veronica home. Bruce made noncommittal remarks since that dinner date was a complete blank to him.

THE WAS NOT WEEK

Bruce then saw again on the calendar that he had a note for this Monday to firm up the details for the second date with Veronica. He called her at once and they set up a movie and supper for Tuesday. Brue asked her to repeat her address. Veronica said to Bruce last Thursday was romantic to her since they took what she always wanted a horse drawn ride. Veronica also said how nice Bruce was in refusing to come up to her apartment. Veronica also remarked how much she enjoyed the hug and kiss and Bruce had to fake all knowledge and succeeded.

Bruce spent the rest of this now Monday calling and visiting friends to try to fill in the last week gaps. He spent time with Sue and Ted and being very careful. He discovered details re: Veronica and the dinner. Bruce learned that Veronica was 26, never married, a mid-level manager at fire and casualty insurance company, doing well financially, and she enjoyed current movies and was an avid reader. At the dinner, Bruce and Veronica found out they had similar tastes for books and had read many. Bruce feeling more confident, kept the second date with Veronica, never alluding to the first date but using his information so that they had an enjoyable time together. Bruce wanted to take his budding relationship with Veronica slowly. Bruce was concerned about the "Was Not Week" and worried that he might have a brain injury. Bruce did have an appointment with his family doctor, George, and did tell him about his totally lost wee. George could not rationally explain how Bruce functioned as usual but had zero memory of that week. George scheduled several tests but there was no medical cause discovered. In medical literature there were similar occurrences but this proved unhelpful. Brue was persuaded to have visits with a psychologist, Harold. The six visits were helpful but the "Was Not Week" mystery was never explained.

THE WAS NOT WEEK

The prime mystery was how Bruce could function and all of his routine matters such as eating, painting, hygiene actions, appointments; his successful first blind date with zero memory and also providing no clues to all those individuals he interacted and conversed with was never determined. This proved to be such a rare form of amnesia that scholarly essays were written but shed no light at all on the central mystery.

As time went on Bruce accepted that there would be no viable answer so he went on with his life since he had no other option. Bruce concluded it was a one-time freakish thing that happened to him and he, having no choice, would live with it. Matters became serious with Veronica and Bruce told her about the lost week. Veronica offered no answer since she had no answer but told Bruce she loved him and knew they could have a very good life together. Bruce took this remark at face value and proposed to Veronica. They did marry four months later. Bruce had an outstanding career as a free lance artist and Veronica became one of the first female CEO's of a major insurance company. Bruce did have rarely recurrence of "The Was Not Week" amnesia of one or two day duration. He functioned with no problems so that other than Veronica and his health care providers, no one knew. They had two children, Sadie and Richard so far as is known, the children had no amnesia episodes.

The mystery of "The Was Not Week" was never solved.

KINDNESS AND PEACE

This is a short fiction story - a "what if?" fable.

For a magical 24 hour time period all over Earth kindness and Peace prevailed. Deaths still occurred due to disease and accidents. However during that 24 hour span no injuries or deaths occurred due to violence or war.

Everyone, friends, foes and strangers only displayed kindness and peaceful words and actions toward everyone encountered. No harsh, mean, or vile language was used. No nasty letters to the editor were written. No domestic abuse - verbal, emotional or physical happened. Those that were bitter and sworn enemies the day before embraced each other like long lost relatives.

In all schools, religious organizations, political gatherings, public and private places only kind words and deeds prevailed. There was no malice shown by anyone.

Everyone sought out those who needed help of any kind and offered and did help. It was by all accounts and measures "Peace on earth and good will to men and women and children." Religious groups went out of their way to embrace other groups sincerely. Throughout the world the religious sayings took place both in words and deeds such as "Do unto others as you would have them do to you." "Judge not lest you be judged." "One who is without sin may cast the first stone." "Love your neighbor and others as yourself." "Give help to the poor, the needy, the disabled and infirm." "Give of yourself to aid others and you will be rewarded."

The media reported this phenomenon worldwide and good news was reported.

One of the most unusual facts was there were no naysayers -- no pessimists -- no skeptics. There were only optimists. Of course people all over the world wondered if this was true and most hoped and prayed it was true and would last.

KINDNESS AND PEACE

Alas, this was a 24 hour one day event and the next day's animosity, hatred, negative emotions, wars and violence recommenced. But in actuality many people due to that unique event changed their beliefs and feelings and desired to have a kind and peaceful earth. And they started slowly but surely to use their voices and feelings and intelligence to change their small part of the world for the betterment of all.

It took much strife and sorrow to change minds and attitudes but this started to happen.

Since this is a fable, it took exactly 323 years, 4 months, two days, three hours, and 14 minutes for kindness and peace to be everywhere on earth.

SURVIVOR

Jimmy was born in a breach birth with the umbilical cord strangling him. The doctor and health care providers knew what to do and succeeded so that Jimmy was born alive. He was in the category of a "blue baby" and extraordinary measures were immediately taken to continue saving his life. Those measures worked and included several blood transfusions provided by Jimmy's father, Daniel. Jimmy survived.

An unusual occurrence happened when Jimmy, then two, was sleeping. Jimmy was bitten by a dangerous spider. His mother, Susan, had woken at about the same time and was worried. She rushed into Jimmy's bedroom and turned on the light and saw the spider. Susan used a cloth to capture the spider. Susan and Daniel rushed Jimmy o the nearby hospital. A few days before that hospital had received a new shipment of anti-venom for spider bites. Due to the fast action of his parents and the presence of the anti-venom serum and the very rapid action at the hospital, Jimmy was treated and survived.

When Jimmy was five, he was visiting with his parents, relatives who lived in a five story apartment building and they resided on the fourth floor. Jimmy, ever curious, somehow fell out the open window and was falling to serious injury or death. There was a woman, Rose, admiring the landscape who caught Jimmy and partially broke his fall. A neighbor, George was very close by and he intervened to help Rose and Jimmy was unhurt and survived.

Jimmy, now 7, went to summer camp near a lake. Jimmy had been swimming well since he was four years old. Everyone at this camp was instructed about the lake, swimming and sometimes undertow. One sunny day in July, Jimmy was swimming with several others when a sudden undertow happened. Jimmy with knowledge and instinct continued swimming with the flow of the undertow and was able, using his stamina and swimming ability, to beat the pull of the undertow and swam to the beach and survived.

SURVIVOR

A virulent strain of the flu hit the United States when Jimmy was 10 years old. His parents had not yet had Jimmy vaccinated that year deciding to wait till flu season was imminent. They had followed the same procedure in prior years and no one in their family ever had the flu. This year, however, the flu hit very early. Jimmy was taken to the hospital and given a powerful vaccine. This hospital specialized in treating the flu strains and while Jimmy was there for four days he received very good care. Jimmy survived the flu which that year killed many elderly and young victims.

The next year when riding with his parents and in the back seat on a booster seat and with his seat belt attached, their vehicle was struck by a vehicle whose driver ignored the stop sign. Jimmy was sitting behind his mother, Susan, and their vehicle was struck on the passenger side. Susan suffered a concussion and bruised ribs. His father Daniel, had a compound fracture of his right leg. Jimmy was also taken to the hospital for various bruises and to be checked. Jimmy was released the next day while both his parents, Susan and Daniel, remained hospitalized. Jimmy stayed with relatives and once again survived this serious automobile accident.

SURVIVOR

During the summer that Jimmy was thirteen, he, his parents, and others went fishing on the lake. The weather was balmy and the fishing was great. With no warning a major squall came up and everyone knew there was serious danger. The boat had equipment to send out SOS signals and Daniel used the radio equipment to also ask for help. An unusual combination of wind, the squall, and the lake currents combined to capsize the boat and all were thrown overboard. The six persons including Jimmy's uncle Roger and his two cousins Ralph and Sara, twelve year old twins, all had donned life jackets when first boarding the rented boat. For three terrifying hours, they all clung to the upside down boat. Jimmy was actually the best swimmer and he had taken several water safety courses. Jimmy helped his cousins to stay afloat. He also played a part in saving his mother Susan when she hit her head when first entering the water. The U.S. Coast Guard rescued them. Susan suffered nausea but did not have a concussion. Jimmy was praised for being the hero but he did not crave publicity so the story of this heroism received scant coverage by the media. Jimmy survived.

In November of the year that Jimmy turned 14 and was in 9th grade, a horrible event occurred. A former student, 20 year old Richard, came into the school and started shooting. Richard shot five students, one teacher and the custodian. Two died and the others survived their injuries. Richard approached Jimmy and pointed his pistol at him and pulled the trigger. The pistol misfired and when Richard tried again, the pistol jammed. Jimmy, believing he had no option, tackled Richard and with the aid of another student, Jonathan, and a teacher, Samuel, subdued Richard. Jimmy had practiced self-defense and in the melee broke the right wrist of Richard which never healed. The police arrived and took Richard into custody. Once again, Jimmy was hailed as a hero but again he sought no media publicity. Jimmy was elated that he survived.

SURVIVOR

The very next year, Jimmy now 15, at home when doing a woodworking project building a small cabinet for his mother, Susan, suffered a cut on his left hand. Jimmy washed the cut and put on a bandage and continued to complete his cabinet project. Two nights later, Jimmy could not sleep due to pain and discomfort to his left hand. His parents rushed Jimmy to the hospital, where he was diagnosed with a viral infection. Antibiotics and other treatment were done but to no avail since Jimmy was unfortunate enough to have been infected by what was commonly referred to as a "superbug." Jimmy, neither awake nor asleep, started to consider his life and the various times he had survived.

Jimmy was happy with his life and wanted to achieve his dream and passion to be an architect. Jimmy also thought about Diane, a vivacious redhead in his class, whom he was planning to ask to go to the next school dance. He believed in himself and remembered the eight events he had already survived so far. He wanted for sure to survive this horrible infection. Jimmy believed in free will and refused to think that fate or destiny played any part in his survival episodes. Jimmy was not willing to just accept that he had survived those occurrences just to fall victim to a "superbug." The doctors who observed Jimmy and his struggle did not use the word "miracle" but thought that Jimmy was a true survivor who beat this infection. Jimmy while recovering thought about his future and whether a new event would happen which he again would have to survive. Three days after entering the hospital, Jimmy walked out fully recovered from the "superbug" infection. Jimmy knew the next day at school he would ask Diane to go to the dance. He did and they went. Jimmy survived.

SURVIVOR

Janet, 33, finally thought it was time to sort out and dispose of her grandmother's personal property. Nothing had been done for over 15 years. It was time since her mother Irene died two years ago and Janet had just completed all legal matters regarding Irene's estate and last week had given away the last belongings of Irene.

Ruth, the grandmother, had no furniture remaining. All her clothing was disposed of. There were three boxes and one had old papers, tax returns, insurance documents etc. and that box contents were shredded and went into the rented dumpster. The second box was sorted and there was kept some old mementos and jewelry and these were given to various relatives with Janet retaining some. The third box contained a treasure trove. There were two partially completed manuscripts -- one clearly an unfinished autobiography and the second an incomplete period fiction novel. There were several journals with poems and snippets of songs. Janet decided to keep that box in its entirety but the box itself was mildewed. Janet obtained a plastic container and transferred everything to that container. In doing so, she found a small red box. She opened it and saw a rather plain bracelet. She wondered why that was not with the other jewelry. She placed it on her left wrist and out of the air a whispering voice started to speak:

"If you, the wearer dares to do so, you can undo one and only one regret in your past." "Please know that if you use this power, there usually are unforeseen consequences." "Twelve others before you have exercised this undoing regret power with ten of them having dire and horrible results." "In the other two, good and bad results cancelled each other out." "You have ten days to exercise this power or it cannot be used by you."

"This message will not be repeated." "Think long and well."

SURVIVOR

The message ended. She thought this was a trick. Examining the red box, she found under the lining a document which detailed the twelve previous users of the bracelet. To say the least, ten tales ended with death and destruction. Perhaps this was the result of poorly thought out choices in selecting the regret to undo.

Janet after reading these tales of woe at first decided to do nothing but the next two days in thinking about the matter concluded that she would first make a master list of regrets in her past to be undone. She made the following list, not in order of importance:

UNDO ONE REGRET

1. Giving up for no valid reason her virginity at age 15.

2. Shoplifting but never caught for 18 months when she was 19.

3. Her lack of judgement in having an affair for five months with a married associate professor at college.

4. Deciding just two months before her marriage to Scott to break up with him.

5. Her initial complete disregard of her mother's symptoms which if paid attention to might have prolonged her life.

6. Her desire to further her career so she refused to consider having a child which was desired by her husband, Steve.

For the next three days she thought of little else but those six regrets and if totally undone what the result would or could be.

In thinking about the loss of virginity, she realized this would have happened later and she could not see what good result for her would be if that regret was undone.

With the second one of shoplifting she regretted this and was ashamed but could not visualize if undone how her life would change or be better.

With regard to her affair she did not feel that undoing that regret would be beneficial to her presently.

She thought that going ahead with the marriage to Scott would clearly change her future in unknown ways. She thought undoing that regret, if regret it really was, was far too iffy a situation. Her present marriage to Steve would most likely not occur. There were too many changes to consider undoing that regret. Further she thought beyond the reasons she had at the time to break up there probably were major hidden reasons to break up with Scott.

UNDO ONE REGRET

She did think long and hard about the regret regarding her mother. In the first place it is totally unknown whether undoing the regret re: her mother would have prolonged the life of Susan and she died some two years ago. Undoing that regret most likely would not have altered Susan's pains and might have resulted in more medical heroic measures taken which in turn might very well cause even more pain to Susan.

With regard to the regret of not having a baby she concluded that she had so far had a good marriage and a successful career. She and Steve had married four years ago and there still may be time to have one or more children.

She decided that there was no needed reason to exercise the power to undo one regret in her life.

Susan had a best friend and first cousin, Amy, so after the ten days had passed she confided in Amy and gave her the red box, the bracelet and the document.

Amy was curious and put the bracelet which then whispered the same story except changed the number to thirteen.

(The story of Amy and succeeding possessors of this bracelet must wait for future telling). (Likewise the tales of the previous twelve).

BATHROOM – TABLOID - LAWSUIT

Sally, a woman of indeterminate age, was generally healthy except for a week when out of the blue diarrhea struck three times. Two of the episodes were relatively mild and occurred in her home.

The third episode was a major disaster.

Feeling well, and believing the diarrhea matter was behind her, she went to an upscale store seeking to buy slacks and sweaters. She had found slacks and tried them on and was well pleased.

Suddenly without warning she knew she had to get to the store bathroom fast. She left the three pair of slacks on a table and rushed to the bathroom. She barely made it. The worst was soon over and she reached for the dispenser of toilet tissue. To her dismay only four small narrow pieces came out and they shredded and curled. At that stage she was frantic and actually called for help to no avail. She hobbled her way to the other two toiled cubicles and the same thing happened. No matter what she did she could only obtain four small narrow toilet tissue pieces. The toilet tissue dispensers all froze up. She had a good sized handkerchief and with that and the toilet tissue she made do. She then, annoyed and frustrated, found that the soap automatic dispenser was out of order and the second one only provided a miniscule amount of soap. The faucets seemed to have a mind of their own and only squirted out little cold water and she did not have time to let the water heat up. Even more annoyed and just wanting to get out of the store and go home, she tried to use the hand driers. No matter what she tried she could not get these to work. Whether they were damaged or there was a special trick to operating them, she did not know. She finally dried her hands as best she could on her dress. Holding her head high, purse in hand, she left the bathroom.

BATHROOM – TABLOID – LAWSUIT

She was confronted by two salesclerks, one who is in a loud voice asked her what she was doing regarding the slacks. It was summer time and her dress was stylish and sheer. It was obvious to all that she had no suspicious bulges such as shoplifted clothing. The other salesclerk saw a stain on the back of her dress and let out a series of guffaws. A few customers were drawn to this confrontation and soon general laughing occurred. She was by then in tears and needed to leave. There was no violence but she felt intimidated by the sales clerks. Thereafter she had no reoccurrence of the diarrhea problem and was ready to forget the whole depressing experience. She vowed to herself to avoid that store.

For an unknown reason she picked up at another store while waiting a local tabloid and read with dismay an article stating that Mrs. S, a well known hair stylist had a funny thing happen at a store and showed a security camera photo of her back with a noticeable dark stain on her sheer dress.

For the next three weeks she felt humiliated since there was a running story about her mortifying experience. Anyone in that small city knew who the mystery Mrs. S was.

Her husband, Harold, had given solace and comfort to her but she seethed with indignation. Harold suggested she have a consultation with an attorney. Sally called the Bar Association and promptly had an appointment with an experienced knowledgeable attorney, David. He told her that the tabloid could not be successfully sued because the story they published was basically true. To prove that the tabloid deliberately targeted Sally out of malice was impossible.

BATHROOM – TABLOID – LAWSUIT

Sally did tell David the very embarrassing story of the store bathroom and defective at least to her toilet tissue dispenser, soap dispenser, faucet malfunction and total failure of the hand driers. David pointed out that this type of negligence and/or product liability case would be very difficult to prove and would entail need for expert testimony. Experts are very expensive, he asserted. Further in Federal court if she lost the case she may very well have to pay the attorney fees and costs of the defendants. The final point was that although Sally suffered humiliation and distress she was not physically injured and her possible legal damages minor. He said he had a good private detective who at some expense could determine if there was proof of the confrontation with the two store salesclerks so that the store could be sued. She paid David a retainer fee and the amount needed for the P.I., Brian, to do an investigation.

Brian knew an employee, Jim, at the store involved and Jim owed Brian a favor. Jim said it was widely known at the store that that incident happened and it was captured on a security camera, both video and audio. Tapes were usually recycled every 48 hours but one of the sales clerks had a duplicate of the nine minute tape saved separately and several copies were made. Some of the salespeople and other store employees often spent their break times viewing that tape.

Brian prevailed on Jim to get a copy of that tape. David called Sally and she with Harold came to his office and viewed the tape. The tape also contained extensive verbal remarks from many store employees ridiculing Sally by name.

David believed this tape and conduct of the store employees was actionable and with the agreement of Sally and Harold he filed suit in State court against the store. David promptly used discovery and the tape record actions and words of the store employees was established.

One of the store lawyers suggested a settlement whereby Sally would have a lifetime supply of toilet tissue. Another suggested the lifetime rental use of a toilet tissue dispenser, an automatic soap dispenser and functional hand dryer.

Realizing the potential public relations debacle, the upper management made a very good financial settlement. This involved suspending seven employees, providing a well worded written apology to Sally, destruction of all tapes, and a lucrative store based purchasing card (which Sally and Harold used but never abused).

The store also installed better dispensers of toilet tissue, soap, water, and hand driers throughout their stores.

NOTHING

Jake, 21, was in his third year at the University. He was an engineering student and since he had taken additional courses for the past two summers was on track to graduate with a major in mechanical engineering. He took an advanced English course since he wanted to enhance his communication skills. At the end of April there was an assignment to write a 500 plus word essay on any subject. He selected the word/concept "Nothing."

Jake had recently broken up with Sarah, also 21, and a fellow student in the English class. She was taking a course of study leading to a double major of Creative writing and Professional Grant writing. Up to three months ago they were compatible and happy, partially due to the existence of being students with mutual sexual benefits. They had been together for almost two years and neither had any serious ideas of marriage. They were both focused on their goals and career choices. Starting three months prior, Sarah had gained about ten pounds and was unhappy with her body image. She took up smoking; he abhorred the smell of tobacco; he did not like to be in a smoke environment. In the past, he had changed his dorm assignment because a roommate smoked. He had no true medical allergy to cigarettes but intensely disliked smoking and smokers. He was appalled at Sarah who for the first time in her life took up smoking and sometimes with anger told Sarah to quit smoking. She did lose over 12 pounds and was trim and svelte and really like her body image. She resented what she saw as a controlling and dictorial attitude and told him so. She tried to moderate her smoking when they were together but the remnants of smoking clung to her. Therefore, they mutually broke up.

Jake felt down and in effect nothing since the breakup still affected him leading to his choice of "nothing" as his essay subject.

He was somewhat lazy and did not want to do extensive research for his essay.

He used two different dictionaries for a definition of "nothing":

NOTHING

Nothing means ultimate negativism -- no past or trace of past -- something of no importance or value -- person of no value -- nonexistence. Also zero -- nothingness.

At that moment that fitted Jake's mood exactly. He ran across the word "nihilism" which seemed to him a result of feeling nothing. He found out that nihilism is a philosophy term meaning denial of the existence of any basis of knowledge or truth. In politics nihilism means to destroy all government or social actions to start over from scratch. This concept leads to violent terroristic revolutions. Finally the belief that existence is worthless and all laws and institutions he destroyed.

He gave a great deal of thought and wrote an essay which rejected nihilism but to some extent recognized the idea of nothing. He received an A minus for this essay.

He was called upon to read this 730 word writing and with passion read this. He added that by choosing this topic it led him to rethink his personal life so that now he not only rejected personally anything to do with nihilism but also now believed in optimism and a positive attitude in his own life. Sarah was present but did not change her mind and felt that Jake wanted to control her and she believed that cigarettes and coffee would maintain her image of herself and her body.

His rendition did resonate with another student, Joy, and filled her mind with the truths expressed by Jake. Joy, 20, a communication major desiring to help to shape TV news being her passion and career choice, warmly congratulated Jake. He was attracted to her and asked her to go to lunch and she accepted.

They found a rapport together.

Joy some five years later, asked Jake to marry her and he said "sure" and they married.

DONATION AND WARRANTY

The computer not quite four years old had outlived its usefulness for Mary, who was a computer programmer for IBM. She was 27, married for two plus years to Salvatore, the same age, who was a junior professor at a local college, teaching introductory Botany.

Mary went on line and found a business so she could purchase a six months warranty for the Dell computer. Mary planned to donate the used computer to an abused women's shelter where she had volunteered for the past eight months and wanted that non-profit organization to have a viable computer. Denise W., the manager of this shelter was pleased to have a working computer and she asked Roberta and Denise A. to take instructions from Mary so they could readily utilize the computer.

Their initial job was to type in and save an inventory of the assets of the non-profit including furniture and equipment. Within two days they completed this chore. They moved on by listing all residents of this shelter with relevant personal information. Denise A. particularly was adept with computers and performed the majority of the entry of data.

A week or so later the computer froze up and Roberta called the warranty company. Bruce came there about two hours later and soon had the computer working again.

Bruce mentioned to Roberta and the two Denise's' that Mary was very astute to have bought the six month warranty.

Bruce scheduled two times to come and clean and test the computer to make sure it was fully operable by the time the warranty period expired.

Bruce, a mature 46 year old divorced individual, at once liked the older Denise W., the manager and asked her to go to dinner. Denise W., 43 years old, who had never married, took a chance and accepted this invitation.

DONATION AND WARRANTY

The next evening Bruce took Denise W. to a Chinese restaurant. They spent an enjoyable evening both liking the variety and taste of the several entrees, sweet and sour pork; spare ribs; wonton soup; and a joint eggroll.

They especially enjoyed the hot tea served in the dainty cups. Denise W had been working on a book of poetry and Bruce related that he had a passion for contemporary poetry and actually had done readings. He invited her to his next poetry reading. She came and was enthralled when Bruce became a different person displaying an Irish baroque animated when reading two short poems. This was a laid back reading without a fixed agenda.

Denise W., having imbibed a Rum and Collins, was persuaded by Bruce to use the open mike system. Denise somewhat nervous, first explained that she had no written out poem but went on to relate with enthusiasm a somewhat lengthy narrative poem. She grew more confident and there was laughter from the twists in the poem as told by her.

Spontaneously, Bruce grabbed Denise and swung her around, hugged her, and then gave in public a truly passionate kiss which Denise not only accepted but returned with fervor.

Both Denise and Bruce, when that evening was ending, told each other that this was by far the best time of their lives.

Denise W. the next day, sent a hand written letter to Mary reiterating what a great donation the Dell computer was to the shelter and to her personally. She expressed the thought that the providing of the warranty with the donation was truly inspired. Denise W. revealed in that letter to Mary that she believed she was in love with Bruce, and that was the result of the warranty.

DONATION AND WARRANTY

Six months later Bruce and Denise W. were married at the shelter and on display prominently was the donated computer with a now expired warranty. Bruce as one of his pledges to Denise W. said, "I am the warranty for the donated computer". Bruce for the next six years till that computer was replaced was the living warranty. Denise loved Bruce for himself, his passion for poetry and his generous spirit. And Bruce reciprocated with elan and passion.

EVERY AND VEXING

Harold became aware of his sociability problem when at age four he was trying his est to articulate his thoughts. In those early years, he sort of stuttered or was not able to say what was in his brain as his words were garbled and largely misunderstood. As a defense mechanism Harold retreated so that he became "silent Harold". In pre-school, he would share toys and play with others. He was basically an obedient child.

Often when he would have preferred to utter his thoughts he felt alone and stymied.

As time went on, he learned to practice speaking in front of a mirror. Harold became known in school as one who did not raise his hand nor volunteer answers. But he was known to be the most prepared student since if the teacher assigned certain portions of the book to be read and studied, Harold would read and study the entire book. With regard to math if instructed to do five of twenty problems, Harold would do all twenty.

Often teachers knew if no one else in a class was prepared to expand the class knowledge Harold was. Sometimes Harold was labeled by other students as a "teacher pet" but the truth was that Harold used his intelligence to over prepare in all subjects to make up for his inferiority complex and his painful inability to initiate or carry on a conversation.

This vexed Harold no end. Harold did very well on written tests. Since through High school due to time constraints it was rare to have oral tests, Harold never found out whether he could be articulate in that setting.

Harold did have a group of friends since he was a loyal comrade and he would never betray or tell tales about his friends' infractions so long as they were non-violent towards people and basically rebellious conduct. If a fellow student needed any help with lessons Harold would be there to help. Harold would not write essays or papers for others nor would he play any part in actual cheating.

EVERY AND VEXING

When Harold was sixteen, he heard of a plot by three older students to grab and attack Sally, then a Senior and a year older than Harold. It was late in the school day and he could not warn Sally. Harold went to the locale where the ambush was to occur and he had a flare gun. When the three hoodlums arrived with Sally, Harold fired several times with the flare gun and using a menacing attitude while wearing a stocking mask to distort his facial features, he succeeded in causing the three to run away after Harold had hit one with a bat and broke the right wrist of one and hit another on his left shoulder fracturing it. Sally told Harold that she believed the three had learned a lesson and did not want to call the police. Sally had a few bruises on her arms and strangely was not frightened. Sally was religious and expressed forgiveness of those who meant to harm her.

Harold escorted Sally home without revealing his identity and waited to see that she was safely inside her home

The two culprits based on their injuries were unable for some time to play on the basketball team. The one with the injured wrist was disabled from playing sports. Harold made a point to send all three a written document detailing their scheme and a photograph of their attack. None of them ever bothered Sally or any other female student again.

Harold also volunteered at the local boys and girls club and taught remedial basic science and math lessons.

Harold in his junior year took for credit a culinary year of study. His motive was that he wanted to eat better while attending college and he believed this course would be beneficial. In fact, Harold became a good cook and his study helped him in many ways throughout his life.

EVERY AND VEXING

The one bad result was that Harold only received a C and his grade point average fell so that he ended up fourth in his class. Harold timidly asked three fellow female students to attend the senior prom but was refused. Harold did not know that two of them were in serious dating relationships and the third was hoping without success that the star of the football team would ask her out. Harold did not go to the Senior prom.

Harold had lost his father, Fred, when he died of a massive stroke when Harold was 13 and his mother lost her battle with ovarian cancer two months before Harold graduated.

Harold was an orphan and had no siblings. There were two elder aunts who showed no interest in helping Harold. His best friend, Jim, convinced his parents to allow Harold to reside with the family. Actually Harold used the family of Jim as his official residence for college and his higher education and continued to list that address when he obtained his position as a nuclear engineer specializing in nano-technology.

Harold met Sally again when he was 29 years old and Sally was hired as a research assistant at the company where Harold was the best employee. By this time, Harold had several patents and was more than well off financially.

Harold had spent all his a spare time to overcome his speaking problems and used every method to cure this vexing problem. Harold by this time was very articulate and could easily converse about his scientific endeavors and books and music subjects. He was known to be a good social conversationist.

Harold met Sally and she knew him from high school. Harold helped Sally to be acclimated to the company. One evening Sally broke down and told Harold about her disastrous marriage and her bad divorce. She told Harold that her ex was harassing her and if this kept up she would have to quit this position and flee elsewhere.

EVERY AND VEXING

Harold did not tell Sally but he followed her and discovered Brent, the ex was stalking her. Harold used a stun gun to subdue Brent. Harold took Brent to secluded forest area and forced Brent to strip. Harold had an axe and with one blow cut a large branch in half. Harold disguised told Brent he had one chance to live and that was to leave this area and never return. Brent was frightened and agreed to leave Sally alone

Harold meant what he said and to prove his intent destroyed the I phone and valuable watch that Brent had. Brent resigned from his job and vanished forever.

Harold using every new skill he had conversed with Sally and eventually told her that he had admired and cared for Sally all the time since high school.

Harold and Sally dated for some time and often went dancing. He always found some subject to interest Sally. He not only was articulate and not shy but was very persuasive. They did fall in love. Their employer had no policy against fellow employees dating or marrying. Following their marriage and the birth of their two children, Maria and Danielle, they had outstanding careers with the company.

Harold's vexing speaking issues were ended in every way. Harold's new problem was being articulate too much and so much so that quite often Sally had to tell Harold "Shut up and kiss me". Harold complied.

SHOWER INSPIRATION

Amy, a 29 year old part-time stand- up comedian was seeking fresh material for her five minute act. Amy felt she had exhausted her family and she was loathe to create fictional family members. She visualized if she did so, they would become real and want to visit her.

At any rate, she was in some hurt because of the breakup with Walt for the fifth time and so she wanted to believe what she thought of as the forever breakup. It occurred two nights ago and Amy did not want to relive all the turmoil in recreating the vicious dialogue just to have an audience laugh at her misery.

Amy thought about a hot and cold shower and since she had little to do other than to be clean in body, she disrobed and turned on the shower. Amy was almost happy when the hot spray hit her until she came quite close to falling. Amy now was living alone since Walt had moved out for the eleventh time. Often he would move out to practice and get Amy's goat. One time, after such antic, Amy deliberately soaked Walt's side of the bed with sodden towels but that did not play out as anticipated since Walt rolled over onto Amy and they had a very wet miserable sexual encounter. Amy never tried that stunt again and she had a wet dream for several nights thereafter.

Amy recovered from the almost fall with minor unseeable bruises (since Walt was gone and no one replaced him yet) in intimate places.

Amy thought "Some good can come from a shower fall. I know I have a peg to rely on for my stand-up act or this time it will be a sit-down routine."

Amy wrote the following so she could practice her delivery of the shower story:

SHOWER INSPIRATION

"I took a shower so I could have a clean act. Dirty thoughts and remarks need a clean body. I did fall in the shower thinking what I will not do for art and comedy. I came up with the idea of installing a trapeze bar in the ceiling over the shower. It would be able to be lowered and raised and swing in all directions. The trapeze bar would be padded so that it could be changed to match my mood and décor—green for spite—white for purity—red for anger—brown or tan for dull--orange for thrill—purple for passion."

"This swinging bar would be a valid safety device. I could and would use it to swing nude in the shower and think of erotic matters. I will yell as Tarzan might have."

"A major drawback presented itself—I could get all sweaty and need more showers and swing some more getting sweaty over and over. "Consider a naked woman swinging, getting sweaty, and showering. Another problem is if there are water restrictions. What if this endeavor led to true water shortages and others had to forego showers?"

Amy while drying off, contemplated calling Walt and inviting him over so he could install the trapeze bar but instead thought about asking two male friends over to do the same, George and Henry.

Amy had one other prurient thought, "Two may be better than one". On that happy note she dressed leaving to practice her new shower comedy routine.

FEW AND UTILITY

Gary was five years old and one of few savants. His ability started a few months after birth when his parents, Isaac and Josie noticed that Gary seemed to recognize faces. At first they believed his actions were usually what babies do. It soon became evident that Gary had a special talent. One early example was the nurse, Dorothy, who was on duty when Gary was born came to the house two weeks later to deliver an item that Josie had left in her hospital room. Dorothy and Josie had friends in common.

Gary upon seeing Dorothy cooed and smiled and waved his hands. All there knew that Gary recognized Dorothy.

Gary consistently recognized everyone he came into contact with even ones he saw only once and only had a fleeting three second glance. When he was able to talk Gary spoke clearly and totally accurately with their full names. Gary was never wrong.

Gary started preschool with 14 other children when he was three years old. There were over 150 children at that pre-school and within one week Gary could call everyone by their full names and recognized with no errors every child. Gary did likewise for all of the staff; all visitors; all parents.

It became a sort of game and when Gary recognized the face and names of all who ever came to the preschool, the media ran several stories about this unusual talent.

Gary could and did do the same thing with all relatives he came into casual contact with; everyone in the neighborhood and everyone at any store or retail establishment.

He went to a show at the Radio City Musical Hall, a famous show on Broadway and was requested to see about 500 people attending the show and to hear their names. Gary was brought up to the Stage and correctly named every person in that audience, although without Gary being aware, they all changed their seats.

FEW AND UTILITY

The ability of Gary with regard to face and name recognition was well-known. The FBI came to see Gary and his parents. The lead FBI agent, Susan, said they, the FBI, felt that Gary could be a great utility to them.

Susan produced large albums of known criminals' mug shots and asked Gary to look at them for as long as he wished. Gary took about a half hour to rapidly scan over 1,000 faces and names.

Susan then spent two and half hours using the help of two other agents and a named the page and Gary had instant recall without error of every name and face.

Susan and the other two FBI agents left as true believers in Gary and his extraordinary talent.

Over several years, the FBI hired Gary to perform face recognition endeavors. They would show Gary, for example grainy photographs of a bank robber and Gary promptly identified both the face and name of the suspect. He had the opportunity to see at least several thousand mug shots. Of course, sometimes Gary had never seen a mug shot of the suspect and could not identify him or her.

Gary, after graduating from college, opened a consulting service and aided law enforcement including FBI; DEA; Homeland Security in utilizing his unique talent so that each year well over 300 suspects were identified. Most were captured and convicted.

Gary rarely testified in Court utilizing his talent for the investigative phase of criminal matters.

Gary did appear when he was 26 in two consecutive trials, both ending in guilty verdicts.

June, a paralegal in the office of the prosecution, observed Gary at trial. June, acting upon a dare by her sister, Darcy, after Gary testified at the second trial, asked Gary out for dinner. June was a year older than Gary. Gary had little romantic encounters in his life and was entranced by this pretty redhead and agreed.

FEW AND UTILITY

June took Gary to a Mexican restaurant. When the waiter came to take the order, Gary, as was his habit, said he wanted no cheese in any part of his meal and his selections were very limited. June loved cheese and ordered several items with a cheese compote. Gary told June he hated cheese and always believed he would be very ill if he ate cheese. He said he did not mind watching other people eat cheese but had difficulty understanding the "why" of cheese consumption. Gary and June had a good time.

This led to several more dates. In accepting Gary's proposal of marriage, June mentioned she would she would make every effort to have non-cheese home for Gary. Gary responded that he loved June and she could fill the house with cheese as long as Gary could refuse forever to not eat any cheese.

GOING AND TENACIOUS

Barney, the four year old dog, part Rottweiler and part shepherd, was not in his usual place in the outside kennel at the home of the Darbys', Kate, the mother; Ray, the father; Julie, the 19 year old daughter, Ray Jr., 17 years old; and Toby, the youngest son at 15.

This was moving day for the Darby's, the large moving van having been loaded and departed a half hour ago.

Ray and Kate had loaded both vehicles the evening previous and only last few items had to be stored.

The plan was that Ray and Toby would be in the 2011 SUV with Barney in the back. Kate, with Julie and Ray Jr. would drive the 2012 Ford Taurus. The route to their new home about 800 miles away had been mapped out. The two vehicles would meet up at various locations on their journey for meals and sleeping. They had GPS and several cell phones so they could stay in communication.

The trip scheduled for three days was also a semi-vacation. Now it was departure time on a crisp June day at 6:45 a.m., the precise time to leave, and no Barney. The house had been sold and the new owners were to be there the following day.

All five tried to find Barney but no luck. Ray talked to his neighbors: Josie, a widow and also Sam and Arlene and asked them about Barney. Kate alerted her sister, Angie to the Barney snafu.

Toby mentioned that the last few days Barney was roaming around and said that Barney might have found true dog love with Francy, a mixed shepherd and collie. Toby went to the house where Francy lived but no one was home.

They had Barney since he was a tiny pup and they all loved Barney. Julie suggested that she and Ray Jr. would stay behind and find Barney and then catch up with the others. Julie had two months left before her driving license would be reinstated and Ray Jr. was somewhat inept in driving the 2012 Taurus. Both Ray and Kate refused and at 7:40 a.m. having exhausted the Barney search, drove off.

GOING AND TENACIOIUS

Barney earlier that morning found Francy, abandoned and pregnant since her owners decided to get rid of Francy and her unwanted puppies (it had been determined that there was a litter of three expected in about two months.)

Barney had an acute sense of smell and with Francy beside him was following the direction of the departed moving van.

Barney and Francy showed up at the new Darcy home 34 days after Ray, Kate, Julie, Ray Jr., and Toby had arrived. The travails that Barney and the pregnant Francy had with their travels and adventures remained unknown.

At their new home, the Darcys had a large back yard set up for a dog or more. They had all been grieving for Barney and did not want to replace him.

All were moved by the tenacious actions of both Barney and Francy. Barney had lost a little weight but Francy was well fed.

The Darcy's believed that Barney had for sure bonded with Francy and had protected her and fed her and their to-be born puppies. Two days later Francy gave birth to one male and two female puppies. The Darcy's knew that Barney was a unique dog. They loved all five dogs and provided for them. Barney and Francy barked and protected them. Barney and Francy barked joy when the puppies were named; Travel, later nicknamed Trav; Journey with nickname of Jo; and Tenacity, with nickname of Ten.

HEWN AND SALVER

John, now age 35, had been a timberman for over 15 years and had been married to Anita for nine years. They had triplets, Amelia, Georgia, and Susan, age 7. In Some two months they expected a son, who they would name Roger.

John had a successful business with three experienced employees, Dave, several years younger than John, and Abner and Simon, many years older. Their business with John as sole owner was named "Do you need a tree cut down today?" specialized in clear-cutting woods so that a residential subdivision or business or a school could be built.

At the present time the business – "DYNATCDT" –had a backlog of several months since John was very efficient, honest and fair in pricing projects.

John had a home workshop with many woodworking tools and equipment. He had a hobby of making tables and cabinets from some of the trees he cut down and salvaged. John liked to use oak, walnut, cedar, and cherry.

John had an arrangement with a lumber company which he supplied with hardwood trees so that the sawmill would provide John with finished lumber. John also had a side endeavor in dismantling unneeded barns. He often kept some barn wood so he could construct cabinets from old barn wood.

Georgia, the daughter, showed an interest in wood working and she often was with John when in his home workshop. Georgia wore at all times safety goggles and used tools and equipment only when John was present. She liked using the plane and sanding the cabinets and tables.

One early evening, John asked Georgia to go with him to make a delivery of cedar and walnut logs to the sawmill. Georgia admired a round large walnut log and told her dad "Why not have that walnut log hewn and sawed so that several circular pieces can be available in different widths? I saw a book with decorative platters called salvers. I could design some and we could use these walnut circle pieces to make unique sets of salvers.

HEWN AND SALVER

John talked to Dick, the sawmill manager, and the walnut log was sawed so that about 100 separate pieces were produced from that 45 foot straight log.

A week later the circle pieces were delivered and John, Georgia, Amelia, and Susan stacked them.

Georgia selected three of them and John shaped them into serving platters, or salvers. Georgia encouraged Amelia and Susan to cooperate using the convincing argument that the salvers could be art objects. Susan was creative in drawing and use of colors whereas Amelia liked to design. This family project resulted in three different sized and shaped salvers being produced.

One salver was taken to their school for show and tell and won universal acclaim. A second one was entered in a local museum art contest and won first prize in the artistic dishware category.

That was start of a new business called "Triplet Salvers".

This internet business was very successful. Each salver was a work of art and was one-of-a kind.

The profits from this business provided enough funds for college education for the triplets and their baby brother, Roger.

Triplet Salvers enabled John to sell his timber business to his employees and to turn his wood working hobby into a business. John specialized in making unique furniture using a mixture of hardwoods and salvaged barn wood.

The triplets with help eventually from Roger grew "Triplets Salvers" into a regional successful business and all four children did the marketing and advertising; the artwork for the salvers; and with help from John and his business created the distinctive shaped salvers for sale and profit.

ITALIC AND RESPONSE

Mary learned to print at an early age. On her fifth birthday she received from her Uncle Thomas a beautiful book written in italic printing/writing. All letters sloped right. Soon Mary was practicing italic printing and writing.

Mary had received several birthday presents from distant relatives. Mary had thank you cards to send out.

She had a skill in both printing and writing. Instead of cursive, Mary wrote thank you notes in italic.

This went well and the relatives praised Mary. Each holiday and on special occasions, Mary combined cursive and italic printing and writing so that all those receiving these missives were enthralled. The local news paper interviewed Mary and had a cultural story about the artistic writing skills of Mary.

Mary also had both a journal and diary and wrote every day. Mary also started to write in her distinctive style interesting short fiction stories.

When she was ten a publisher contacted her parents, Henry and Jane, and Mary had her first published book.

Mary throughout her schooling starting in kindergarten only used italicize printing and writing. The standard was cursive and Mary when confronted by teachers would use lovely cursive but much preferred italic. After Mary's acclaimed book was published widely, school authorities not only permitted Mary to use exclusively but required her to do so.

Mary became an acknowledged prodigy for her italic printing and writing. Mary became a featured star on childrens' television. Her several books including three re: poetry and seven compiling short fiction stories were for years best sellers.

At ago 20, while in her third year at college, Mary fell in love with Marco, an Italian exchange student. Marco had wavy coal black hair and hazel eyes. Marco was athletic and played both college soccer and football and he was very handsome.

ITALIC AND RESPONSE

Marco, when the mood took him, spoke in Italian to Mary and she understood it since she was well-educated in Italian, Spanish and German. Mary was one of the few who could actually use Latin to converse. It was rare for Mary to utilize Latin in conversations but Marco sometimes could keep up with Mary.

Marco did not care to print or write but only used his Dell computer for his writing.

For his 22nd birthday, Mary found a software package that was compatible with Marco's Dell so that Marco could write his college work in italic.

Mary and Marco were in love until Marco revealed he had a wife and young child in Milan, Italy and was duty bound to honor his family commitments. Marco took the issue of adultery cavalierly since he was in America.

Marco had a saying, not in italic, "What occurs in America stays in America" and further "Italy and America are two different worlds". Marco displayed this adultery attitude as years went on when he was in Paraguay, Ecuador, Zambia, Netherlands and many other non-italic writing nations. Rosa, his once a bride, stabbed Marco in an unmentionable place ending Marco's amorous conduct forever and Rosa thereafter divorced Marco on the grounds he could no longer successfully perform his Italian obligations as a husband.

During those years, Mary indulged in affairs of the mind, heart, and body. Mary had from one of those liaisons, twins Louis and Lisa. Mary did encourage her twins to learn cursive and italic and they responded with ardor doing so.

Mary decided at age 29 when the twins were almost four to try marriage for a change. She compiled a list written in italic of men she would pursue to marry.

Mary married Mark, a 32 year old film editor. It was later said that on her honeymoon, Mary wrote exotic erotic italic poems to Mark but this could never be independently verified.

JUSTICE AND QUARRY

An all-points bulletin was sent out for Jacob, now twenty years old. Jacob had lost both parents several years ago to the usual combination of alcohol, drugs, and crime. His mother, Sadie, was sentenced to 12 to 20 years for her participation in robberies. His presumed father, Ivan, was serving federal time (15 to 30 years) for being convicted as a drug dealer and was the prime suspect in three execution style murders.

When Jacob was nine he entered the foster care program with typical results. By age 18, he had been in four different foster homes. His juvenile record was lengthy. Jacob, however, did very well in school and had a 3.65 grade point average. Jacob received a scholarship offer from MIT due to his abilities in Math and Physics but since he was incarcerated at the time he was to be on the campus of MIT, he forfeited this chance for normality.

Jacob had a girlfriend, Trixie, also 20, and a part-time beautician.

Jacob, despite being unemployed, wanted to get an expensive bracelet for Trixie. Having no money he stole six bracelets thinking there would be a choice for Trixie. Jacob was caught on the security cameras.

Jacob ran to Felix, a fence, and sold four bracelets for $150.00 Jacob hurried to the beauty salon and Trixie was just finishing her shift. Trixie took Jacob to her one bedroom apartment. Jacob proudly showed Trixie the remaining two bracelets and Trixie not able to choose took both and strutted around wearing both bracelets.

As Jacob was telling Trixie about his escapade, the radio announced that Jacob was the quarry of the APB and the announcer said justice would prevail.

Jacob told Trixie to hide the bracelets and find some way to alter them. Jacob was aware that he would be captured and his family would be three for three.

Jacob considered fleeing but came to the conclusion to surrender. Jacob did so and was given a sentence of 4 to 6 years in the nearby penitentiary. Trixie never came to see Jacob and hooked up with Sam who later that year beat up Trixie and stole the bracelets and her extensive makeup kit.

JUSTICE AND QUARRY

MIT had an outreach program and enrolled Jacob as a freshman. Jacob was sent educational materials and he spent most of his time in prison studying. He passed each test in various subjects and scored 100 percent in the varied math and science courses. Jacob was the best student in the MIT outreach program and he earned a B.S. degree in five years with a double major in mathematics and physics.

Shortly thereafter, Jacob was released on probation. He accepted a full scholarship at MIT and within three more years had a Master's degree. He was offered a position on the faculty at MIT and he eagerly accepted this.

Some faculty members opposed Jacob and resented him. This ended when Jacob received a large grant to study for two years: The interaction of nano physics; cellular mobility; and quantum calculus and probability curvatures.

Jacob did so well at MIT that he turned down an offer to be the administrative head of the departments stating he wanted to continue working in his fields. Jacob wrote many articles published in scientific and math journals. He attempted to write a scholarly book but was convinced it not only would not be for the general public but would be ridiculed.

Jacob in his early thirties met an acclaimed ballerina, Joyce, 29, and who was to shortly become the assistant director of the internationally famed ballet company.

Jacob and Joyce spent a few hours talking about their pasts. They both had a love of books, music and dance. Joyce revealed to Jacob that she had been in a foster home for a brief time when her parents were recovering from serious injuries.

They both had chickenpox, measles, but not mumps. They both had what is known as scarlet fever and fully recovered.

Jacob spent much time with Joyce and although she was good at math, most of what Jacob did was beyond her. They enjoyed working on crossword puzzles and if either was at a loss regarding gifts, they gave each other books of puzzles.

The most compatible of their likes was that both read and enjoyed countless mystery books.

JUSTICE AND QUARRY

Jacob told Joyce his criminal past was behind him and he asked Joyce to take a leap of faith and marry him. Joyce did not wait and accepted the proposal.

Their marriage was happy and they never lacked for anything to converse about and they always retired in the evening knowing they spent their time well.

Joyce had a miscarriage and a still birth but later two children blessed their union, named Diva and Euclid.

SECURITY AND SEX

Carol, 25, was about to exhaust her unemployment compensation benefits in four weeks when she went to apply for a position at a small company owned and managed by Ted, 33.

Neither Carol nor Ted had ever married and at this time neither was involved romantically with anyone. Carol had lost her position as s paralegal when the law firm she worked for was in a breakup situation. Carol had clerical skills. Ted gave Carol an intensive interview.

Ted told Carol he would hire her as s paralegal, if in fact his present paralegal, Dorothy, did get married in three months as planned and relocate to another state.

Ted had a prosperous business in the import / export global world. Ted had an internal legal department dealing with trade and international issues and also patents and copyright matters. Ted employed outside law firms on occasion but most legal work was done in house.

Ted was not willing to hire Carol now since she would need very little training. Ted was also concerned that Dorothy as she had done in the past would at the last moment cancel the wedding.

Carol was very unhappy and said if this paralegal position did open up and she was still in this area she would accept that employment.

Ted then told Carol he wanted her to consider a different proposal – that of marriage. Carol was astounded but Ted asked her to listen to his idea. Ted said he had been burned before when he thought he was in love and there was no good result.

Ted reminded Carol of all the questions he asked in the interview and her ready answers. He said "We are very compatible in our values about end of life matters; raising of children; money issues; likes re: music, theater, movies, entertainment and sports, etc. ". Carol agreed this was all true.

SECURITY AND SEX

Ted asserted and Carol agreed that most marriages which started with sexual and emotional attraction failed when real life issues occurred.

Ted asked her to think it over. He stated that Carol would have that which she wanted true security regarding money and the use of the same. Ted also told Carol that marriage and regular sexual life would bring to an end , Carol having a series of one night stands and also end Ted's so far fruitless pursuit of what he termed false love.

Ted made the argument that many if not most marriages succeeded because both parties compromised and accepted reality that the marriage model where sex and security were in effect the tradeoffs. Of course, if one party to any relationship was an abuser; controller; heavy drinker; drug addict serially involved in adultery — or a myriad of other personality defects these would prevent a successful relationship from evolving and enduring.

The last thing Ted said was "You know, Carol, we both want to marry and both of us want a family with children. I cannot say now that I am in love with you nor that in fact I will ever love you. Personally, I do not know what love as a pure emotion is and I have never felt it. Carol, I know in your mind you agree with these ideas of love. Finally, take a chance on security, sex and possible or probably enduring happiness." Carol left, saying she would give real thought to this proposal.

Carol had a habit of making lists regarding important matters and she composed a master list detailing pros and cons regarding Ted's marriage proposal.

Paramount for Carol was the fact that she feared poverty and wanted to work at a meaningful paralegal position and she when seriously considering the issue of security knew she would be happy if she had real financial security.

SECURITY AND SEX

In four days, Carol came to the conclusion and called Ted for a second interview. They spent three hours discussing in-depth issues regarding money, security, children, Carol's need to be employed and other matters. Ted said he wanted Carol to be happy and have a paralegal job and stated that if Dorothy left, there would be zero problems in Carol being hired, regardless of her decision regarding marriage.

One matter they discussed in a thoroughly candid fashion was matters of sex. They covered all aspects. Both believed in being monogamous and both swore oaths to never consider adultery. Ted told Carol that if either had future regrets or for any reason did not want to remain married that a truly amicable divorce would occur. Both Carol and Ted wanted the same things from marriage and life.

A detailed contract was prepared providing financial security for Carol. Carol did tell Ted that financial security was very important to her and Ted provided this. But, added Carol, she realized that emotional security was equally important and she believed that Ted would provide this also.

Carol was employed as the paralegal. One month later they married. Throughout their marriage they had true emotional security; a sexual life to be envied; a very happy marriage with three children, Donald, Alice, and Timothy, all of whom had good professional careers and marriages. There was ultimately a total of 11 grandchildren. Carol retired as paralegal on her 62nd birthday. Ted never retired. Ted and Carol never spoke the words "I Love You" to each other but everyone who ever observed them knew they had the best kind of love – the real kind.

KARMA AND POSITION

Joseph, 27, was a freshman at the community college. He was taking a two-year course to be .a nursing assistant. This community college was noted for a good graduation rate and employment. Joseph had served in the U.S. army for about the eight years until he was medically discharged due to shrapnel severe wounding of his left arm. He had to some extent recovered as much as possible but was left with a 50% disability. He was awarded a modest army pension. Joseph believed he could have a viable nursing career.

In one of the class, Joseph was called upon to state his view of karma/fate vs. free will. The associate professor used the word Karma, and gave a dictionary definition: "bringing inevitable results on oneself by action."

Joseph responded by telling the tale of the last battle he was in when an ambush occurred in a mountainous area of Afghanistan several months ago. Joseph related details regarding the fire fight and that two of his buddies died there. In addition six others including Joseph suffered serious wounds. Joseph said he believed in and accepted the free will concept. After all, he volunteered and served 3 years in that war zone. He had other injuries in combat and came very close to death on more than one occasion. Joseph expressed his view that there was no Karma or fate in what he lived through. Joseph stated he felt fortunate to have left that war area with what he considered not a minor disability but one he could live with.

By the end of his story, Joseph was seen by fellow students as an optimistic individual and one who had lived through "hell on earth" and survived with his personality intact. He was not seen as a wounded soldier with post traumatic stress problems but as one who desired to rejoin society as a normal person. The professor and other students applauded Joseph.

Joseph had kept a wartime journal but had never revealed or discussed its contents.

KARMA AND POSITION

A fellow student, Beth, 25, in the same nursing program, was divorced and raising a daughter, Sally, age three. Beth had federal and state aid in going to this community college under an outreach program to defeat poverty. Both Joseph and Beth were doing well in their studies. The divorce had devastated Beth since her husband, Harold, disappeared leaving debts for Beth to deal with and provided zero child support. Beth received food stamps, housing and heat assistance but no cash funds. She had a part-time job at a local pharmacy. Her family has helped her financially.

Beth talked to Joseph and invited him to join a start up writers group focusing on memoir writing. Joseph had a part-time job working at a grocery store.

Joseph, wanting to know Beth better, accepted the invite. The group met once a month for two hours at the public library and the mentor was a college professor. Everyone in this group desired to write their memoir and was learning to do so. Joseph brought his journal to the meeting and read brief excerpts. All encouraged him to start writing this war time memoir. Beth in particular told Joseph that his entries were well-phrased and enthralling. She took the position that not Karma or fate controlled him but he owed it to the public to show what some elements of war were really like. Joseph agreed and during the following year wrote his memoir. He sought help from the group and they were supportive. Someone had contact with a book publisher and a junior editor came to a meeting and listened to Joseph reading a moving portion of his story.

His memoir was published and was on the New York best seller list for 12 weeks. There was an option from a cable television company but no movie was ever produced – basis was not that Joseph's story was not good material but there was a lack of high drama and gore in it. Joseph was asked to turn this into fiction but he refused stating that this memoir was real and it would be a profound mistake to trivialize it by fiction. Joseph did obtain a nursing position. (Joseph thought this as free will and not Karma or fate).

KARMA AND POSITION

Beth at the group meetings was reluctant to relate the feelings that she had during the years of an abusive marriage, the divorce, and its aftermath. Joseph made several overtures to Beth in asking her to take a chance and date him and he strongly urged her along with other group participants to write her memoir. Joseph's main point was that this would be good for Beth to release her innermost feelings and this would be a catharsis for her. Beth did actively participate with the group by writing and reading amusing short stories relating to her daughter, Sally.

Joseph helped Beth when she needed a ride home sometime. Beth did not believe that there would be a benefit to her letting Joseph into her and Sally's life since she still thought that Joseph was damaged by his wartime experiences and she did not want to take any more chances with affection and relationship. Beth was still troubled by her failed marriage and how blind she had been in evaluating her ex, Harold, and she believed that she lacked the ability to see men clearly enough.

Joseph did not give up and finally Beth said she would have two dates with Joseph. The initial date would be determined by Joseph with the second one being a dinner at their apartment with Sally present. At the first date, Joseph took Beth to a movie which was somewhat enjoyable and a dinner afterward. Both Beth and Joseph were nervous and somewhat uncomfortable. They both tried too hard and the date as a whole was only okay.

Joseph came to the apartment of Beth and Sally and they were both more relaxed. The dinner was tasty and they enjoyed the company of each other.

Joseph got along with Sally. Sally was rushing and tripped over a doll and fell breaking her left arm. At that moment Beth froze but Joseph did what needed to be done. He stabilized the left arm of Sally and took charge by driving with Beth holding Sally to the nearby hospital. Sally fully recovered.

KARMA AND POSITION

Beth realized what a good person Joseph was and she removed every thought that Joseph had PTS and felt warm feeling for Joseph. Over the next few months they dated and fell in love. (Again, Joseph knew this was not Karma or fate but resulted from their exercise of free will).

Soon after they graduated and had positions in nursing they married in a church wedding with Sally being the flower girl. Two years later, twin boys named Zack and Isaac were born making their family complete. Their marriage had ups and downs but it endured because they both needed and wanted each other and had mutual love. Without questions, this family had a great life together.

Joseph and Beth accepted the position that free will prevailed and their lives were not in any manner controlled by Karma or fate.

www.ingramcontent.com/pod-product-compliance
Lightning Source LLC
Chambersburg PA
CBHW081146170626

46809CB00010B/3109